12/21/

Dear Jeannie,

Are you as thrilled as I? I can't stop bubbling... especially when someone I adore asks me to autograph her book. I mean *you*!

Enjoy, and tell me what you think.

Love,

Anita Jacobs

Where Has Deedie Wooster Been All These Years?

Where Has Deedie Wooster Been All These Years?

A NOVEL

ANITA
JACOBS

DELACORTE PRESS/NEW YORK

Published by
Delacorte Press
1 Dag Hammarskjold Plaza
New York, N.Y. 10017

Lines from "Hiding" by Dorothy Aldis: Used by permission of the Putnam Publishing Group.

Manufactured in the United States of America

First Printing

LIBRARY OF CONGRESS CATALOGING IN PUBLICATION DATA

Jacobs, Anita.
Where has Deedie Wooster been all these years?

Summary: Fourteen-year-old Deedie, an aspiring writer, dilly-dallier, and worrier, chronicles the often humorous but frequently painful process of growing up.
I. Title.
PZ7.J148Wh [Fic] 81-65493
ISBN 0-440-09461-5 AACR2

To Mike, Sue, and Larry

Part One
Lost

I'm hiding, I'm hiding, and no one knows where,
For all they can see is my toes and my hair. . . .

DOROTHY ALDIS

~~A friend named Allie~~
~~A girl friend~~ named Allie Loomis
who ~~was~~ in my ~~Junior~~ High
~~Once told me the trou~~

A girl friend named Allie Loomis who was in my Junior High once told me, "The trouble with you, Deedie, is you don't recognize Bullshit when you see it."

If anyone reading this book happens to run across Allie, I would appreciate it very much if you tell her that I recognize it now.

You might find her at Hero-Burger. Not in the front or on the sides but in the back, Where More Goes On, if you know what I mean.

You could also tell her for me that she was right about Thomas Jefferson. He did get Syphilis from his Slaves. I found out it was going around and I'm sorry I doubted her.

I would of told her myself, but unfortunately Allie dropped out of school for getting Pregnant.

Thank you.

1

One of my biggest Worries was that I would get my Period when I was in School and not have a nickel for th

Excuse me a minute. I want to stop right here and let you know what I look like. I don't know about you but I can't really get into a book till I know how the person looks who's telling the story. I've been surprised too many times and didn't like it. For instance I could be reading about a girl and just by the way she talks I get this very clear picture in my mind that she's got dark brown hair and dark brown eyes and she's around average height and things like that. And all of a sudden the Author says:

The wind whipped Linda's flaming red hair back

from her fragile shoulders. Her blue eyes filled with tears. Her slight frame quivered from the cold. Her tiny feet . . .

I hate that. And sometimes I don't get this Information till page 20 so I have to start the book all over again with flaming red hair, blue eyes, fragile shoulders, slight frame, and tiny feet in my mind instead of all that other stuff I imagined. It's not that I mind so much that Linda never grew past Munchkin-size, it's just that I'd rather get that straight right from the beginning and not waste all that time, if you know what I mean.

Okay, so I'm pretty tall for my Age and I have this straight black hair that is very thick and never looks right so I keep it short because that way there's less hair that doesn't look right. I also have a Cowlick in the back that makes me look kind of Dopey and once I got so disgusted with it that I took a scissors and cut it off clear down to the roots. I don't have to tell you what a mistake that was because when my Cowlick started to grow in again it looked like I had these skinny black straws sticking up out of the top of my head. It's all back in now, thank goodness, and I look more normal. I forgot to mention that I have black eyes to match my hair.

I'm kind of scrawny although I did go through a Fat Period when I was younger but that didn't last very long. I'm scrawny again except in the Bust which may be a blessing some day but right now I don't see the advantage.

Personally I think I'm kind of sad-and-blah-looking. For a long time now I've been practicing to raise one eyebrow because I think it would give me an Interesting Personality Trait but so far I can't do it.

Oh, yes. You've probably noticed that I hate Commas and I like Capital Letters even now that things have straightened out a little. I think that has something to do with my Personality too. Mom says it's my way of "defying authority."

Mom's right.

You've got enough to go on, I guess, so I'll start over.

I

One of my biggest Worries was that I would get my Period when I was in School and not have a nickel for the machine in the Girls' Room. I wouldn't exactly say it was my Number One Worry because I had so many I wouldn't of known which went first. It so happens that the very first time I got my Period I did get it in School and I carried on like nobody's business. I knew what it was and all that, but it's the kind of Experience where you prefer to have your Loved Ones around you and not the School Nurse (who went through almost a pack of Marlboro Lights before she could calm me down). But I'd better tell you who I am first.

My name is Deedie Wooster, I'm fourteen years old, and I want to explain right off that this isn't a Mystery. I mean from the title you might get the impression I was actually missing, but I wasn't. Don't think I was another Patty Hearst or something and that my Father was tearing his hair out trying to find me. My Mother either. In fact I was the only one who didn't know where I was.

This book is mainly about my Observations and all the things I Worried about when I didn't know where I was which was the first fourteen years of my Life. Of course I've pretty well established where I am now which is in the Ninth Grade at Einstein Junior High, Calderwood, New Jersey, Zip Code 08602, United States of America, the Planet Earth, the Universe. There's a Nuclear Plant under construction close to where I live so this address could be only temporary, you understand. As if I didn't have enough to worry about without that.

Don't look for any Plot in my book because there isn't any. I would of liked to have a big Climax in the last Chapter but so far I haven't thought of one. Like I don't end up a big Rock Star or Movie Star or Television Personality. I did pretend to be related to Kristy McNichol once and got in a little trouble over it but I don't make up stories like that anymore. Now that I know where I am, so to speak, I don't lose myself quite so often.

"Where *are* you, Deedie?"

That was the kind of question that made me wonder where I was. I mean, I could be in the Kitchen, for example, worrying about what would happen to me the next day and Mom would say, "Where *are* you, Deedie?" I would like to of said that I was right there at the Kitchen table and if she'd of opened her eyes she would of seen me which was true but somehow I knew that wasn't the right answer.

I couldn't blame Mom for asking though. Most of the time I wasn't sure where I was either.

That's how I got the idea to call my book *Where Has Deedie Wooster Been All These Years?* It's what most Teachers would call a Thought-Provoking Title and though I don't happen to agree with Teachers very often I think they're right about titles. They're very important.

Titles I mean, not Teachers.

2

I almost called my book *D. Wooster: Her Worries and Obsvs.* because I once saw a couple of books with that kind of title in the library at School. But I was afraid you might ask yourself, "Who's this D. Wooster anyway and why should I care about her Worries and Obsvs.? I've got enough of my own!" To tell the truth if I saw a book with that kind of title on a shelf today it would stay on the shelf. It would be just the kind of book Mom would give me for a Christmas Present.

"Look, Deedie," she'd say, "here's a book about a fourteen-year-old and I bet you'll like it because she sounds a little bit like you. *All* fourteen-year-olds have Worries, Deedie, so don't think you're alone in that Department. Maybe we could read it together, what do you think, Dear? Well *I* think you should do more Reading, I really do. If you did more Reading maybe your Grades would go up because let's face it, Darling, your Grades could stand a little Improvement. And for Goodness Sakes, Deedie, don't look so Miserable! These are the Happiest Years Of Your Life!"

You can see why I didn't like that title.

Then I thought of *Too Many Geraniums On My Back* because Geraniums had something to do with why I didn't know where I was and it's kind of grabby as a title. But that might of suggested an Addiction to something, like Cocaine, you know, and I'm not into Drugs.

But I definitely think titles should have Eye-Appeal. A good title can make a person want to read what you've written even if what you wrote is on an entirely different topic. Because by the time the person is on the second page he doesn't care if the book is about something else. He's so interested that he keeps reading anyway.

Like *Fear of Flying* for instance. Most everyone knows that *Fear of Flying* isn't really about airplanes, it's about Sex. But I'll bet a million people started to read that book thinking it would help them stop being afraid of airplanes and when they got to the second page they found out they were wrong. But it didn't matter because they were also interested in Sex and were naturally Pleasantly Surprised.

It so happens that in *Fear of Flying* you find out it's about Sex on the *first* page because the Chapters in that book have titles too and the title of the very first Chapter is called "The Zipless F--k" (I hope you can read between the lines) and right away you can tell that book probably isn't about airplanes or even flying, for that matter. I know because Mom hides it in her night table and I've read parts of it. I'm positive Mom picked it up because she *is* afraid to fly but the Author got her even more interested with the title of the first Chapter so naturally Mom continued on. That's how the Author gets twice as many people to read her book, the ones who are afraid to fly and the ones who like Sex. (Frankly it came as a surprise to me that Mom was interested in both.)

That's what I mean about titles.

One more thing, otherwise you may not believe I wrote this book myself. I ought to tell you that I want to be a Writer (when and if I grow up, that is) and I happen to have a very good Vocabulary. When I was seven years old my Uncle Freddie gave me a book called Roget's Thesaurus. That was right after my brother Ritchie died.

Uncle Freddie gave me that Thesaurus because

he knew how much I liked to write. And maybe he was trying to keep my mind off Ritchie. It's got a million Synonyms and Antonyms so you can substitute big words for little words when you want to impress your Teacher with your Compositions. I used that Thesaurus as early as the Third Grade, but the trouble was when my Third Grade Teacher read my Compositions she didn't believe I wrote them.

"Who wrote this, Deirdre?" she asked.

"I did," I said because I did.

"No you didn't," she said. "I want a Conference with your Mother."

Well after a while it got to be a Hassle so I didn't use my Thesaurus as much as I wanted to because who needs a Conference every time you write a Composition. But I'll tell you, try as I did to use little words, I didn't like to, so I finally stopped using my Thesaurus altogether because Writing wasn't fun anymore.

I'm using it again though, and I wanted you to know that. I mean in case you come across a word here and there that isn't particularly Ninth-Gradish, I don't want you to think like my Third Grade Teacher that Mom stuck her Two Cents in here. The only thing she reminded me of was to cut out the Capitals, put in the Commas, and that *would of* and *should of* and *could of* are really would, should, and could *have*. There again Mom happens to be right but I learned a long time ago that if you give Mom an arm she takes a leg, and if I would of let her start making changes here I never would of got past page 1.

Which is why I never finished writing my first book.

3

I'll tell you now about my brother Ritchie dying because that has to do with why I started my first book. But not why I didn't finish it. That was Mom's fault.

Ritchie died when he was twelve and I was seven and believe me, Mom was in a bad way. Daddy was too but he kept up a cheerier outlook for Mom's sake. I knew how he felt though because one night about two months after it happened I got up to go to the bathroom and when I passed my Parents' room I heard a terrible sound. It was Daddy and he was crying in his sleep with awful moans and everything, and I could hear Mom talking to him to make him wake up. I'd never heard Daddy cry before.

But Mom cried in the daytime too and it was so

bad sometimes that I'd get scared and begin to cry myself and think maybe I did something wrong so I would go up to my room and shut the door to Worry about it. Once I heard Daddy tell Mom she'd better Snap Out Of It at least for Deedie's sake and then Mom said that she must of felt more of a loss than Daddy did and she couldn't help it, that's all.

Well how could I remind Mom that I'd heard Daddy crying in his sleep too? I just couldn't. Besides I hated to think how Daddy's crying sounded, it was so terrible. Sometimes I'd wake up at night and listen for it even though I never heard it again. I don't know why I did that but I did.

But no matter how Daddy tried he couldn't cheer Mom up so a couple of Summers later he decided that Mom and I should take a trip to California to visit her Relatives. Daddy couldn't go because he had to work but he said it would be a good Vacation for Mom and me. Of course I knew it wasn't a Vacation, just a way to help Mom forget a little bit about Ritchie but I'll tell you, I wanted to go because at least I wouldn't have to go to the Doctor for the Summer.

The reason I was always going to the Doctor was because Mom got this idea that maybe I'd get sick like Ritchie. The Doctor just couldn't convince her that what Ritchie had wasn't Contagious and that I was all right. I was always being weighed to see if I was Gaining Properly (I was) and I was always going to a Health Lab so they could check my blood to see if it was Normal (*it* was). But they took so much blood from me I figured I wasn't going to have any left pretty soon and what was the good of Normal blood if I didn't have any?

So I started to Worry about my Health too. I mean I began to think maybe Mom knew what she was talking about and I really was going to die like Ritchie. At least once a month Mom would say I had an Appointment for a Check-Up.

"I just *had* a Check-Up!"

"That was last month."

"I feel fine!"

"We'll see."

"Well don't I?"

After a while I wasn't sure myself.

You can see how my Health got to be a real Worry to me which was how I got this Compulsion. I was so sure that I was going to die that whenever I thought about Growing Up I would always add "when and if" but only to myself, you understand. Like when I told you I want to be a Writer and I said "when and if I grow up, that is." I'd have bad luck if I didn't say it. I'm just telling you about that so you'll know when you see it.

My Compulsion was really bad at night, especially if I had a Doctor's Appointment the next day. That Compulsion would drive me crazy then and make me do weird things. Like I'd make these deals with myself. For example I'd think if I could lie on my back till I fell asleep then the Doctor would find out I was okay. But I couldn't fall asleep on my back. So I'd make another deal. I'd tell myself if I turned over on my stomach my Compulsion would be satisfied but I wasn't sure if I was supposed to turn to the left or the right so first I would turn one way and then I'd turn the other way and there I'd be turning over and over till Mom would finally come in and tell me to Stop Fooling Around and go to sleep. I guess I sound like a real nut to you but if you ever had a Compulsion you know what I'm talking about. Anyway by the time I'd get to School the next day I couldn't keep my eyes open.

"Deirdre Wooster! Where *are* you this morning?"

And giving in to that Compulsion didn't help any because I still Worried about dying. I was so sure I wouldn't live past twelve which was how old Ritchie was when he died that I'd say to myself, "If you can live till you're twelve then you'll live to be an Adult." And even now, even though I'm fourteen years old and the Picture of Health, sometimes I still think, "Well you're only two years past twelve and that's not very much, you could die any day."

That's one reason I was afraid to start any Long-Term Projects. If I was going to die soon then what was the point, if you know what I mean.

But that's not why I didn't finish my first book. Like I said, that was Mom's fault.

When Mom and I started on our trip to California (we went by Greyhound because Mom didn't like to fly, if you remember), she said it would be a good idea if I kept a Diary. Mom knew how much I liked to write too.

"It'll give you something to remember when you Grow Up, Deedie," Mom said.

"I guess," I said. Naturally I didn't add "when and if" because Mom didn't know about my Compulsion.

I started the Diary anyway and I even began to enjoy keeping track of events, remembering it was important to let Mom see what a good time we were having.

But then, and I forget which State we were in, Mom ate two whole pounds of Peanuts she bought at a Restaurant stop and she Threw Up for approximately two hundred miles followed by Diarrhea for the next two hundred. So I wrote about that and showed it to Mom.

"You can't write things like that in your Diary," Mom said.

"Why not?" I said.

"Because people don't write things like that in a Diary," Mom said.

"I do," I said. I happened to think it made the Diary more Personal, if you know what I mean.

But Mom made me cross out that whole Chapter and I kind of lost my enthusiasm for Writing after that. Finally she said: "Suppose I pay you a nickel for every page you complete."

Well that sounded great because I figured if I put in a lot of extra words I'd be a Millionaire by the time we got back from California. So I went back to my Diary and I must say it went very well. I even started numbering the pages by nickels instead of regular numbers. Mom didn't mind that but then she started to correct my Spelling and fix my Grammar and I lost my enthusiasm again. I kept writing though.

But when we reached Arizona this old man got on the Bus and being so old he had lots of complaints about the Bus and the Weather which was very hot. He made some pretty snappy remarks which made everybody laugh and helped pass the time.

"What do you call that stuff when you write what people say?" I asked Mom.

"Dialogue," Mom said.

"Could I write Dialogue in my Diary?" I said.

"Certainly," Mom said.

So I wrote, "God Dammit, Driver, turn up the Friggin' Air Conditioner!" which is what the old man said all the way from Arizona to California where he got off.

That's when I learned that when you're getting paid for what you write you can lose your Freedom of Speech.

I quit when I reached page $10.50.

4

That experience didn't stop me from wanting to be a Writer but once in a while I would think of being something else. Like for a time I thought maybe I'd be a Famous Actress when and if I Grew Up because I'm also pretty good at Acting. I played George Washington's Cherry Tree in First Grade but that's not a good example because the only ones who saw it were the Mothers and a couple of Fathers who were collecting Unemployment and came to pass the time of day.

But in Fourth Grade we did a Play about Christopher Columbus and I was Queen Isabella. We did it in the Auditorium and it was a whole big Production with Lights and all and we put it on at night.

If you want to know, everybody said I got to

play Queen Isabella because Mom made the Costumes and maybe I did get the Part because of that but I was very good as Queen Isabella just the same. But something happened during the Play that made me decide once and for all to be a Writer.

There was this very fat boy named Warren in the class who the Teacher picked to be King Ferdinand. Personally I would of picked someone with a thinner body but Warren's Father built this Throne for the King which believe me was the only reason he got the Part.

If you remember, Columbus needed money and ships for his trip to find The New World and King Ferdinand said no because he didn't believe the Earth was round. Naturally he didn't want his ships and his money dropping off the edge of the World if Columbus got too close. You could see his point.

But for some reason Queen Isabella had a lot of Faith in Columbus and she said the King should give Columbus whatever he wanted for his Journey. The King said no and the Queen said yes, and one word led to another till the Queen got mad and said he'd better, so finally King Ferdinand gave in but not gracefully.

Well when Queen Isabella overruled King Ferdinand and said Columbus would get the money and ships or she would know the reason why, the whole Audience which was mainly kids stood up and cheered for Queen Isabella. You would of thought Queen Isabella gave everybody a couple of days off from School. Then when the kids settled down, Columbus thanked me heartily and left the Stage.

Now King Ferdinand was supposed to get up and leave also because he was very mad that Queen Isabella had the nerve to overrule a King even though he was her husband. That would of left me alone in front of the Audience so that I could get more Applause and naturally after that first taste I couldn't wait to get the rest of it.

Except King Ferdinand couldn't get up. As I said, Warren was very fat and when he first sat down on his Throne he must of sat down on his King's Robe too close to the top of it and when he tried to get up the Robe held him down like he was nailed to that Throne. And the more he tried the more his feet swung in the air. I don't have to tell you I was very embarrassed standing there while fat Warren kicked his fat legs up and down like he was practicing the Backstroke.

So I got really desperate and looked Offstage to see what I should do and there was Mrs. Zucker the Director of the Play waving her arms like she was swimming too. She kept whispering something to me but I couldn't hear her and her face got redder and redder and I froze like a chunk of ice.

Finally she yelled: "Act like a Queen, Dammit! For God's sake, Deirdre, *act like a Queen*!"

Well believe me I was scared and if you want to know, the only Queen I could think of besides Queen Isabella was the Queen in *Alice in Wonderland* whose words impressed me very much when I first heard them.

"Off with his head!" I screamed.

Which was not part of the Play, you understand, so Warren let out this wail like when you step on a cat's tail and he began to howl like anything. But these Second-Graders who were supposed to be the King's Pages must of been more afraid of me because of the ferocious look on my face than they were afraid of the King or Mrs. Zucker and even though they could hardly lift fat Ferdinand out of that Throne they finally did and I was left on the Stage to receive the rest of my Applause.

The kids in the Audience went crazy then and they all said later I was the best Actress they ever saw. But Mrs. Zucker and Warren's Mother and Father didn't even applaud at all and they said I was trying to Steal the Show which I really wasn't, I was trying to Save it.

I decided to go back to being a Writer and not depend on other people for my Success.

5

But I was telling you about my Worries which began at a very early Age, probably Kindergarten. That's when I discovered the importance of Words.

Certain Words had Capitals and even if they didn't I knew they should by the way the Teacher used them.

All Special Activities were Capitalized.

There was Play Time which was when the boys threw the trucks across the room and the girls complained to the Teacher that the boys were throwing the trucks across the room.

Toilet Time was anytime but occasionally the Teacher would remind us.

"Is anyone ready for Toilet Time?"

Naturally everybody said no, they went at home,

which wasn't always true because sometimes a Puddle or Worse would appear.

"Who made the Puddle?" the Teacher would ask. She never asked who made the "or Worse" because usually that was obvious. If you want to know, we knew who made the Puddle too because the one who did it acted very Unconcerned while the rest of us jumped up and down and yelled, "Phooey! Phooey!" Sometimes we held our noses which was more for Dramatic Effect than anything else because frankly there were so many strange smells in Kindergarten it was hard to tell them apart.

But the "Phooey! Phooey!" meant it was time for the next Activity which was Clean Up Time. The girls straightened up the Kitchen Area while the boys threw the trucks back across the room. The Teacher cleaned up the Puddle.

Clean Up Time was followed by Snack Time which was followed by Nap Time.

Nap Time meant you had to put your head down on your table. You had to be ready for Nap Time exactly when the Teacher said you were because that's when she put her head down on her desk too. Personally I think she would catch Forty Winks herself because once she didn't pick her head up for a long time after we did and the boys started throwing the trucks across the room again. And even then she didn't wake up till this boy named

Kenny or Denny or somebody began to holler because one of the other boys was trying to stuff him into the Cubby where we kept our coats.

It was during Snack Time that I found out *I* was a Capital Word. I was a Dilly Dally.

I was eating my Chocolate Grahams which as you know make a lot of crumbs and I was concentrating on pushing all the crumbs into a little pile with my finger. When the crumbs stuck to my finger I licked them off and made my little pile again. Naturally my finger got wet when I put it back in my mouth and that made more crumbs stick to my finger so I licked them off again. I'd found this an excellent way of cleaning the crumbs off my table, sort of making Snack Time and Clean Up Time one Pleasant Operation, so to speak. All of a sudden the Teacher let out this yell that made me knock the rest of the crumbs into my lap. I also stuck my finger in my eye.

"Deirdre Wooster! *You are a Dilly Dally!*"

She screamed that out right in front of the whole Class. I don't have to tell you that I felt terrible. Then she wrote a note and pinned it to my skirt. I knew the note was bad because of the way she pinned it. She was so mad she'd jabbed that pin clear through my skirt into my Underwear and I couldn't participate in Toilet Time for the rest of the day.

Mom read me the note when I got home. She didn't even bother to unpin it first.

> Dear Mrs. Wooster (the note said),
>
> Deirdre is inclined to Dilly-Dally. Can we Take Steps to correct this?
>
> Mrs. Walters (K-1)

Then Mom said that Mrs. Walters said I was inclined to Dilly Dally which I knew already so I went up to my room to Worry about it. When Daddy got home he got the News and I Worried some more. But Daddy only laughed and said that he came from a long line of Dilly Dallies and look how he turned out which made Mom bang the pots in the sink.

When I finally found out what Dilly-Dally meant I wanted to go back and kick that Teacher.

Here's something I wrote in First Grade.

~~Deirde~~ Deedie Wooster
1- I am a Dordler. (Dawdler)
2. A Pokey.
3. A Slow Poke. (Same as Pokey)
4. Just Plane La$zy
5. A Do-Little (Not Doctor)

It looks to me like some kind of Self-Evaluation Test the Teacher must of given me otherwise I don't know why I would of written it. But here's the important thing about it. If you noticed, I'd put all those things which you might call Worries in the form of a List. And when you see what happens near the end of Ninth Grade something will strike you as kind of familiar. I won't tell you any more except you should keep it in mind.

Anyway you can see how impressed I was with Capital Words. Sometimes questions had Capitals too.

"Deirdre Wooster! Don't You Have Anything To Do?"

"Are You Paying Attention, Deirdre?"

"Are You Asleep, Deirdre?"

"Where *Are* You, Deirdre Wooster?"

In Third Grade my Teacher told Mom, "*I* think, Mrs. Wooster, that Deirdre's problem is simply one of Non-Motivation. She doesn't seem to have Any Direction."

Mom said (but only to Daddy), "*I* think she just doesn't Give A Damn!"

I did but it didn't look that way. I mean I wasn't a Behavior Problem or anything, in fact I was just the opposite. I was very good in Class and I smiled a good deal so the Teacher would think I knew what was going on even if I didn't.

"What can you possibly find so amusing, Deirdre Wooster?"

A lot, if you want to know. Since I was very tall for my Age the Teacher always sat me in the back of the room. Sometimes I wondered if she sat me in the back to keep me away from her because I noticed that the kids in the front were not only small they were also very smart. On the other hand they could of been very smart because they sat in the front of the room. I don't know I'm just saying.

Sitting in the back like that it was easy to let my mind wander and I saw things that nobody else did. Like the way the Teacher looked when she didn't get her Bra on straight and everything was sort of lopsided. Or when somebody snuck a Milky Way during Busy Work or when somebody else was writing on their desk when they should of been Listening.

I was particularly interested in Danny Ackerman who kept his hand inside his pants (in the front, if you know where I mean) which was even more fascinating than the Teacher's crooked Bra.

"What *are* you looking at, Deirdre? What can *possibly* be distracting you from your work?"

Well of course I couldn't tell her what Danny Ackerman was doing and besides I knew it really wasn't Danny or anything else in School that was doing the distracting. Ritchie had died already and

Mom had started those visits to the Doctor which brought on all those Compulsions I mentioned and in addition Mom had started calling me her "Little-Two-In-One" which was how she fooled herself into thinking she still had two children and didn't lose any. If you think that sounds like a bad idea you're absolutely right. But I'll tell you more about that later. Anyway, even if I wanted to I wouldn't of known which distraction to complain about so I didn't say anything.

Just before the end of the Sixth Grade there was this big Conference in the School Cafeteria with Mrs. Leopold my Sixth Grade Teacher and Mom and me. As I said, I got rid of one kind of Conference by not using my Thesaurus anymore but Mrs. Leopold must of figured she still had plenty of material to work with.

I guess she invited some of my lower grade Teachers also because they kept popping in every so often to make an interesting point about my work. They threw all these words around like Lackadaisical and Apathetic. Once they were all in there at the same time and believe me it was like a Catered Affair when you get married. I sat a little away from everybody, trying to look like I didn't belong but of course I did since I was the Guest of Honor, so to speak.

I felt pretty bad about taking up their time. Mrs.

Leopold had already changed into this little Tennis dress like Chrissy Evert wears which was her After School Activities clothes. Her eyes flicked from me to her watch to her Tennis racket and I could tell she had more important things to do than drum her long red fingernails on the greasy Cafeteria table. Usually people remembered not to touch that table if they didn't have to.

"Deirdre," Mrs. Leopold said and she let out this long sigh like air leaking out of your bicycle tire. "Deirdre, you *know* you're capable of better work. What shall we *do* with you?"

Well by Sixth Grade the Geraniums had become a problem along with me being a Two-In-One and Compulsive and so on, but naturally I wouldn't tell Mrs. Leopold about anything, especially the Geraniums. Because even if I was Non-Motivated and had No Direction and was Lackadaisical and Apathetic, I wasn't exactly what you'd call Flaky. So I just shrugged my shoulders, first up, then down.

Then everybody shrugged *their* shoulders up and down (the same way I did, I noticed) and hoped I would Find Myself when I got to Junior High next year.

They also said Good Luck but they looked at Mom when they said it, not me.

6

I got very good News in Junior High. I found out I was an Under-Achiever. Don't let that word scare you. It's the same kind of thing as a Dilly Dally and only sounds bad if you don't know what it is.

Mr. Lewis, the Head of the Guidance Department in Einstein Junior High explained it very nicely to me and Mom.

1. I didn't Work Up to Potential.

2. I had some Yet-To-Be-Determined Psychological Block.

3. My Capacity for learning Far Exceeded my Grades.

Mr. Lewis put it in other words for Mom.

"In Other Words, Mrs. Wooster, the results of Deirdre's IQ and Aptitude Tests are *surprisingly* high and indicate a Marked Discrepancy in her actual Work Performance. She could do *excellent* Work *if* we could ascertain the Root of her Problem. I'm afraid Deirdre will continue to Under-Achieve unless she tells us what's bothering her."

"What's on your mind, Deirdre?" Mr. Lewis said. "Are you having trouble Finding Yourself?"

Maybe I should of told Mr. Lewis about the Geraniums or something because somehow he sounded like he knew the answer to that question already and wouldn't mind looking for me even if it took a couple of hours.

"We want to help you Find Yourself," Mr. Lewis said.

"I will," I promised.

"You've nothing to be ashamed of," Mr. Lewis said.

"I'm not," I said.

And while none of us shrugged our shoulders we all politely agreed I was a little Screwed Up.

When Daddy got home that night Mom told him the trouble with me was that I was a Wise Ass which didn't make me feel too bad. At least I was a smart Wise Ass.

But don't think I didn't kick myself for not telling Mr. Lewis about the Geraniums because getting those Geraniums off my back would of been a load off my mind. I'd better tell you about them.

The thing was that Ritchie used to bring Mom a Geranium every Mother's Day. Frankly before Ritchie died I never thought about Geraniums one way or the other. I guess you could say that I could take them or leave them. What I did for Mother's Day was write a Poem. I'd think about that Poem for days before I wrote it. And after I was sure it was perfect I would copy it on good paper using fifteen different colored crayons so it looked very Professional. Like a Card you'd buy in a store if you loved the person very much and Money Was No Object.

But when I was in Third Grade and the first Mother's Day rolled around after Ritchie died I did a weird thing. Don't ask me why because I don't know. Not only that, but I was sorry right afterward. All I could think was how miserable Mom would be without that Geranium from Ritchie. Not because of the Geranium actually, but when the Geranium didn't come because naturally Ritchie couldn't bring it, she would notice Ritchie's not being there even more.

At least that's what I told myself. But to be perfectly honest, when I think back to that day, I remember how Worried I was that Mom loved Ritchie more than me just because he died and I didn't. I really wasn't sure about her loving me anymore at all because she did a lot of crying whenever I was around.

Anyway I took my Allowance and bought Mom a Geranium. I couldn't tell what she thought when I didn't give her my Homemade Poem, if she was disappointed or what. She looked at me kind of funny. Finally she said, "Oh, Deedie, no . . . I—please, you mustn't—oh, Deedie. . . ." And she started to cry.

"I *want* to!" I said. I used a lot of expression because to tell the truth, all of a sudden I knew I didn't want to at all.

But I don't think she knew what was going on in my head anyway because she was too busy crying. Then she said something that I guess was supposed to make me feel good but, if you want to know, it didn't, it made me feel terrible.

"Now you're my Two-In-One, Deedie," she said. If you remember, I mentioned that before. Not many words, but a lot of trouble.

Even though I was only eight years old then, I knew I didn't want to be a Two-In-One. I wanted to be me, and not me and Ritchie at the same time, but it was too late.

That's when I found out I hated Geraniums. They stank, they really did. I'd never noticed before but they had this smell that clogged up your nose and their leaves were very ugly and furry-looking, even hairy. Actually I should of taken that Geranium back right then and there but now that I was Mom's Two-In-One I was afraid if I did I'd have bad luck like Ritchie did and I would die also. The Geraniums became a Compulsion too and I brought them ever year after that.

So there was kind of a War between me and the Geraniums. And don't think I didn't feel Guilty about that because I happened to love Ritchie very much. He was very good to me, even nicer than I was to him most of the time. I still have some great Memories of Ritchie.

I remember Trick-or-Treating with him on Halloween and one time he let me wear his corduroy jeans which were too big for me. They made a swishing sound when I walked. I had to go to the bathroom real badly but Ritchie wasn't ready to go home yet and I finally wet my pants which were really Ritchie's pants and Ritchie didn't even get mad, he just wouldn't wear those pants again. I still have those corduroy jeans up in my closet where Mom can't see them. They're washed of course.

I remember Christmas Mornings. Whoever got up first, Ritchie or me, we would wake the other one up even if it was only five o'clock in the morning, it didn't matter. And we would try to be quiet but we weren't and finally Mom and Daddy would get up too.

After Ritchie died Christmas depressed me. Mom or Daddy would get up ahead of me and even though I'd be awake I'd pretend I wasn't because I found it hard to face them. So I would finally get out of bed and act like I was tired from being up late Christmas Eve.

Daddy would try to make me laugh but Mom always stayed so quiet that Daddy and I would get quiet too. Like we knew we shouldn't pretend to have a good time if Mom couldn't pretend either. We would of felt like we were leaving her out of something.

But most of all I hated opening my Christmas Presents. And I got more and more each year. I guess Mom and Daddy thought if they gave me a Million Presents I wouldn't notice that Ritchie wasn't there, but that was worse because then I didn't have to share anything with him. After a while I hated opening any kind of Presents, it didn't matter if they were for Christmas or my Birthday or just Non-Occasion. Sometimes I kept a Present for days before I opened it. Mom thought it was because I liked the Anticipation of wondering what was inside. It wasn't. I hated getting Presents all to myself.

Especially on that first Christmas when all my Presents from Mom were signed:
Merry Christmas, my little Two-In-One. Love, Mom

I don't think I was an Under-Achiever before Ritchie died.

7

It was easy to spot the other Under-Achievers in my Class of which there were three more besides me. We got Dittos to do. The rest of the kids were pretty smart at least in their Tests but if you ask me they were kind of strange in other ways. For instance there was this one boy who wore a Pacifier around his neck and he sucked on it when he got Nervous. He always got straight A's though, so the Teacher never complained except once in a while she told him to suck a little softer. To me that was as bad as Danny Ackerman who kept his hand where he did as though he Lost Something.

Personally I think keeping your hand in your pants or sucking on a Pacifier is the worst kind of Under-Achieving you can do. Okay so maybe those boys were only making themselves Feel Good but when I want to do that I use my Pillow and I certainly wouldn't do it in front of the whole Class.

So I made Friends with the kids I did Dittos with. Actually I don't know if you would call them Friends exactly because we didn't see each other after School. We weren't such good Friends in School either. It was just that I had no other Friends and they had no other Friends so we were kind of thrown together.

Anyway there was Alexandra Loomis who we called Allie because Alexandra was a mouthful to say and Allie was very small for her Age. Besides she used to punch you in the face if you called her Alexandra. Once she punched Mrs. Vail the Home Ec Teacher except not in the face because Allie couldn't reach Mrs. Vail's face only her stomach. Allie wasn't even sorry she did that because she got to go home for the rest of the day. So did Mrs. Vail. Later Allie stopped punching people in the face till she got to know them better.

Allie also used to let out a little gas now and then but that was only in Seventh Grade. But I liked Allie and I felt sorry for her. She was one half of a Twin and would you believe that when her Parents got Divorced both of them wanted the other Half and nobody wanted Allie so she was put in a

Foster Home? It was easy to see why Allie Raised Hell every chance she got. Allie's Root of the Problem was kind of obvious I think.

There was one boy who Under-Achieved, Dennis Newton. We weren't in that room two minutes before Allie nicknamed him "Fig Newton" and after another two minutes he was "Fig the Fag." When I told Allie I wouldn't call him that she threatened to punch me in the face but she never did. I don't know why but Nicknames were very important to Allie.

And Dennis wasn't a Fag at all. I mean just because somebody was polite and didn't go around pushing everybody out of his way and wore glasses and said "May I?" and "Thank You" and talked about his Father's Beethoven collection and hated Grateful Dead and carried this Attaché Case like he was from the United Nations didn't mean he was a Fag. It so happens that Dennis was very smart. He always read out of these thick books he brought from home even when we did Math but he never told the Teacher how much he knew so he stayed an Under-Achiever. I never found out Dennis's Root of the Problem but if you ask me he knew more than the Teachers and the Guidance Counselor so they gave him Dittos till they knew as much as he did. I don't know I'm just saying.

The other Under-Achiever was Heather Minkin. We didn't see much of her because she only put in an appearance about once a week. And even when she came she sat way over in a corner far away from the rest of the Class. Allie nicknamed her The Ghost. On the days Heather came to School we would ask her where she'd been all week and she'd wait till she was in her corner and then say she'd Run Away or was visiting her Aunt in New Zealand or had gone to Europe with her Father. Mostly she'd say she Ran Away.

But one day I asked Heather why she hardly came to School and she said she was a School Phobic which meant she was afraid of the School Situation. Once you've been in a School Situation it's easy to understand how Heather felt. Frankly I'm surprised there aren't more School Phobics. I thought maybe I could help Heather get over being a Phobic so I told Allie what Heather told me but the very next time Heather came back from one of her Vacations, Allie punched her in the face for Lying about not really taking all those trips. Heather must of written a letter to the Governor or Somebody because she didn't have to come back to School for three weeks after that.

Naturally I was sorry I'd told Allie about Heather's Root of the Problem and I said so.

Allie said, "Bullshit!" which was her favorite word.

I Under-Achieved all through Seventh and Eighth Grade but I was quite relaxed doing it. By the end of the Eighth I got tired of Dittos. I mean the Teacher would give me a Ditto and I would do it and she'd say, "Oh, my, isn't that nice, Deedie, yes, very nice, let's see what you can do with this." And then she'd give me another Ditto which everybody knew was just to get you off her back till the bell rang or you got another Ditto.

Maybe Allie and Dennis and Heather (when she was there) didn't mind Dittos, but I did. I was still Under-Achieving as I always did, and aside from Allie learning not to punch anybody and not letting out gas once in a while she was still an Anti-Social Person.

Heather kept on being School Phobic except she got better at making up more complicated lies about where she'd been when she was absent. She must of forgot she told me her Root of the Problem because the last time she didn't come to School she said she'd been to Kenya and saw the Mau Mau Uprising and I believed her till I looked it up in my World Book and found out the Mau Mau Uprising rose up in 1952.

Dennis started bringing more books to School and those books got fatter and fatter.

I really started to Worry then. We all still had the same Problems we had when we started. If the Problems didn't go away, would we do Dittos forever? Would Allie stay like she was if her Parents never took her back? And there was no way I could bring Ritchie back, was there? So now I was a Two-In-One and I'd have to bring Mom Geraniums forever. If I never told anyone about the Root of my Problem I would Under-Achieve for always and always.

Or at least till the supply of Geraniums ran out.

8

Even when I got into Ninth Grade my Health Teacher had the nerve to say:

"Oh, no, Deirdre. I've been studying your Records with your Guidance Counselor. You don't have to do a Term Paper. Just keep up with the Class Work if you can. Oh, by the way, here's a Ditto."

Boy, did that ever burn me up!

Which is why I don't think Schools should keep Records. I mean it's important that they know a kid's Background in case of Illness or something. Like if a Student is subject to Epilepsy or has been known to Carry Knives, well then I guess Teachers should be aware of that so they can keep their eyes open if a Situation should arise. But I don't think most Teachers look that stuff up anyway so what's the good of Records?

I can give you a good example. There was this girl in my Third Grade Class who had an Epileptic Seizure one day and when it happened all my Teacher did was stand there and moan, "My God, somebody *do* something! Somebody *get* somebody!"

So one of the kids ran down to the School Nurse who finally came and took care of the girl. But then the Nurse and my Third Grade Teacher had a big fight in front of the Class.

"Why didn't someone tell me she was Subject to Seizures?" my Teacher said.

"It's on her Record," the Nurse said.

"Somebody should of *told* me!" my Teacher said.

"Don't you look in the Records?" the Nurse said.

"Somebody should of *told* me!" my Teacher said.

You could see they weren't Communicating.

But just let a Student be a little bit of an Under-Achiever and they put that in the Record and right away the whole World knows about it. What I mean is you'd of thought my Health Teacher would of treated me like the rest of the Class and certainly not say anything stupid like he'd been studying my Records and he knew for a fact that all I could do was a lousy Ditto.

If you ask me they put a lot of things in Records

they shouldn't anyway. Allie told me that once when she was sitting in the Guidance Office with Mrs. Ingleholtz, the phone rang and it was Mr. Ingleholtz, Mrs. Ingleholtz's husband. Well Mrs. Ingleholtz got to chatting with Mr. Ingleholtz and telling him she wouldn't have time to shop for Dinner after School and he should pick up some TV Dinners on his way home from work. And Allie said that all the time she sat there she had to listen to all this Garbage about how Mrs. Ingleholtz wasn't going to visit her Mother on the Weekend because her Mother gave her a headache and she wasn't going to waste a headache on a Weekend, she would rather get one during the Week and stay home from School.

So Allie said she got a little bored listening to the conversation and she peeked at her Record which was lying on Mrs. Ingleholtz's desk. Allie was pretty good at reading Records upside down because she got a lot of practice, having even more Conferences that I did. And stapled right on top of Allie's Record was a Memo from Mrs. Ingleholtz to all of Allie's Teachers. The Memo said:

> Watch out for "Rocky"! This little Pisser packs a Wallop!
>
> Marlene (Ingleholtz)

Since Mrs. Ingleholtz was still involved on the subject of headaches and her Mother, Allie took that Memo right off her Record and threw it away.

If you ask me Mrs. Ingleholtz could of done with a little Guidance herself. I don't know how she ever got to be a Guidance Counselor in the first place. When you went to Mrs. Ingleholtz to discuss your Program you never got anything settled anyway. Because all she talked about were things like the people who got murdered while they were jogging in Central Park or who got killed on the highway that morning or the latest Sex Scandal. Especially after a Sex Scandal Mrs. Ingleholtz would forget why you came to see her.

She wasn't very smart either and I'm not just saying that. She called me down to her Office once to discuss my Grades and we never even got around to talking about me. First she reminisced about the Son of Sam Murders then she made a few thousand Comments on some mass killer they'd just caught in the Midwest. Then all of a sudden she looked on her desk where she saw a Note. "Hm, what's this?" said Mrs. Ingleholtz, then she read the Note out loud.

Dear Marlene (Mrs. Ingleholtz said),

Regarding Keith Berry, Seventh Grade: Please inform his Teachers not to give him a Pass to leave the room. He likes to Roam. He's the Philip Nolan of Einstein Junior High.

The Note was from Mr. Baxter the Principal. Well Mrs. Ingleholtz got real excited and started searching through her File Cabinet.

"Who's this Philip Nolan anyway?" Mrs. Ingleholtz kept babbling. "I don't have Records on any Philip Nolan! Is this a new Student or what? Why doesn't anyone keep me informed on these things?"

Now even though I was the only one in the room with Mrs. Ingleholtz, I figured she wasn't talking to me. And even if she was, I wasn't about to tell her Philip Nolan was The Man Without a Country, which everybody knew was in the Eighth Grade Literature book. The next thing I knew she would of stapled a Memo on top of my Record telling my Teachers I was a Wise Ass and I couldn't afford any more Problems.

So I just told her I would come back some time when she wasn't so busy and that I certainly hoped she would find Philip Nolan before the Principal did.

Anyway that's why I said Schools shouldn't keep Records. If all my Teachers expected me to Under-Achieve, there was no sense in my doing anything at all.

9

Once I was in Ninth Grade I hardly saw Allie anymore. I didn't see Heather or Dennis either but I didn't care about them, I cared about Allie. The only time the four of us saw each other was in Lunch. But even in Lunch Dennis had his nose in a Medical Journal and the only time I caught sight of Heather was when she made a Stopover from the Aleutian Islands. I was going to miss Allie though.

Naturally Mom liked the idea I wouldn't be spending so much time with Allie. "It's better this way, Deedie," Mom said. "Allie is a Bad Influence on you."

"How?" I said.

"She's got too many Problems," Mom said.

"So do a lot of kids," I said.

Which was the perfect time for Mom to say, "Do

you, Deedie? Tell me, Darling. I mean if you don't want to be my little Two-In-One anymore just say so, Deedie, and I'll understand."

But all Mom said was "You can't learn anything from someone with so many Problems, Deedie."

That's how much Mom knew. Because I had actually learned a great deal from Allie, particularly on the Subject of Sex.

It was somewhere around the middle of Eighth Grade and I was home alone. Daddy was working late and Mom had gone shopping with our next door neighbor. I'd done all my Ditto Homework and I was bored with nothing to do. There wasn't even a decent program on TV.

I started looking around in Daddy's Dresser. First I found the cuff links I'd given him the Christmas before, then I found a picture of him and Mom from when he was in the Army. Daddy used to keep that picture on his Dresser but he didn't anymore. I happened to like that picture because Daddy looked really handsome in his uniform and Mom looked very pretty, actually beautiful. I wondered why Daddy didn't keep the picture where he and Mom could see it.

But after looking at the picture for a while I knew why Daddy had put it away and it made me feel sad. Because I realized that when that picture was taken, Daddy didn't know he was going to have a son someday and that his son was going to die before he Grew Up. That made me remember how I'd heard Daddy crying in his sleep a long time ago and I almost began to cry myself. So I put the picture back in Daddy's Dresser and that's when I found this other little box.

I thought it was more of Daddy's jewelry but when I opened the box there were a bunch of rubber rings that looked like rolled-up balloons. I'd kind of guessed what they were because Allie'd mentioned those things one day in Lunch. But when I started to unroll one of them I wasn't sure anymore because there seemed no end to it. I mean it was much too long for what I thought it was and Daddy being just a normal-sized person I figured how could it be one of those things anyhow?

I decided to ask Allie because Allie hung out behind Hero-Burger at night and was very advanced Sexually. Now lots of kids hung out at Hero-Burger at night. Not me because Mom would of had a Fit. But Allie hung out there and she told me that hanging out in the front of Hero-Burger or even the sides of Hero-Burger was one thing but hanging out *behind* Hero-Burger was a different story altogether. The only kids who went in the Back were the ones who were Dealing, or . . . and here's the part I'm talking about . . . the kids who went All The Way, if you get my point. Which

Allie said she didn't do but she hung out there anyway.

But that wasn't the only way I knew how much Allie knew about Sex. She once played a terrible trick on Heather back in Seventh Grade. Allie had come to School one day with some slimy white stuff in a bottle. She told Heather to drink it and it would make something Wonderful happen. Well being a Phobic and all Heather was alway hoping something Wonderful would happen so she wouldn't be a Phobic anymore.

As soon as Heather swallowed the white stuff, Allie shook Heather's hand and screamed, "Congratulations, Heather! You just swallowed *Semen* and you're going to have a baby! Heather's Pregnant! *Heather's Pregnant!*"

Naturally the white stuff turned out to be only Jergen's Lotion but Allie got two days Detention and Heather stayed home from School about two weeks. She must of gone for Tests or something. But you can see how I knew Allie had a lot of Sexual Know-How even before I found out she was a Regular behind Hero-Burger. Otherwise she wouldn't of known about Semen in Seventh Grade and how it could get you Pregnant except not by mouth of course. That's why I asked Allie about the rolled-up things in Daddy's Dresser.

"They're Rubbers," Allie said.

"They're what?" I said.

"Rubbers," Allie said. "You mean you don't know what Rubbers are?"

"Of course I know what they are," I said. "I just thought these things were too long, that's all."

"They have to be long," Allie said. "Don't you know that?"

"Of course I know that," I said. "I just didn't think they had to be *that* long!" Allie could be a Pain.

"Well they do," Allie said. "And I'm surprised your Father still uses them. They're very Old-Fashioned. Doesn't your Mother use Pills?"

"For what?" I said.

"For Birth Control!" Allie said. "Shit, Deedie, don't you know *anything*?"

Then I remembered this Loretta Lynn song, *Now I Got The Pill,* and I knew what Allie meant. In case you never heard it, it's very Catchy.

"Oh," I said. "Those Pills. Yes, she does. They're in her night table next to *Fear of Flying.*"

"Next to what?" Allie said.

"Fear of Flying," I said. "Shit, Allie, don't you know *anything*? It's a book about Sex. My Mother has lots of them. I read them all the time."

"Mm," Allie said. "Bring me some, will you?"

"What, books?" I said.

"No," Allie said. "The Pills. Your Mother probably doesn't need them anymore."

Naturally I couldn't tell Mom why I was going to miss Allie.

10

I should of known more about the Functions of my Body but being such a Worrier I guess I didn't like all these things happening to me that I had no control over. The School Nurse wasn't much help either which is why I put School Nurses in the same category as Guidance Counselors.

You remember I told you that the very first time I got my Period I was in School. What I didn't tell you was that I was only in Fifth Grade and I think you have to admit that's pretty young to get your Period. And even though Mom had told me what it was and what would happen, I didn't give it much thought till the Big Day, and when it actually arrived, if you want to know, I thought my Insides were falling out.

My Teacher had given me a Pass to the Girls' Room and it was while I was in there I first noticed it. I just kept staring at my underpants, investigating what I saw there, so to speak, and thinking that I must of sat down in something and wondering what it could of been. All of a sudden I realized that whatever it was wasn't from the outside, it was coming from me. I mean I'd had a little stomachache all morning but I didn't associate one thing with another at the time.

As calmly as I could I went to the Nurse but the second I got there I got Hysterical.

"Do you have a Pass?" said the Nurse.

I showed her my Pass which I wouldn't of thought she could read because my hand was shaking like anything.

"This is a Pass to the Girls' Room," the Nurse said, "not to the Nurse. Go back and get a Pass to the Nurse."

So I got even more Hysterical and told her what I found on my Underpants and she finally figured out what I was crying about. She called my house but Mom wasn't home and that really made her mad because then she had to take charge of my Hysterics all by herself.

"Didn't your Mother prepare you for this?" the Nurse said.

"For what?" I howled.

"For this Experience!" the Nurse said. "You just got your Period! Didn't your mother prepare you?"

"Ye-e-e-e-es!" I howled some more.

"Then stop Yammering," the Nurse said which I didn't know I was doing.

"I'm bleeding to death!" I explained.

"Nonsense!" she explained back.

She kept calling my house but there was no answer and that's when she started in on her pack of Marlboro Lights. Then my Fifth Grade Teacher came down to the Nurse's Office because she sent him a Note that I wouldn't be back but since he was a Male Teacher she pushed him out to the Waiting Room where I heard her tell him my Problem.

"Don't you have a Film on that?" my Teacher said.

He was talking about this Walt Disney Film that told all about getting your Period. I'd heard about it from the Sixth Grade girls but being only in Fifth Grade I'd never seen it.

"That Film is for Sixth Grade girls only," the Nurse said. "Not Fifth."

"So show it to her anyway," my Teacher said.

But the Nurse was real upset by then because I got my Period before I was supposed to and I guess I kind of interrupted her Schedule so she said she wasn't allowed to show me that Film till I got to Sixth Grade. Then they had a big argument out in the Waiting Room.

"She's only in Fifth Grade!" the Nurse said.

"But she got it now!" my Teacher said.

"The Film is for Sixth Grade girls!" the Nurse said. "She can see it when she gets into *Sixth*!"

"But she got it *now*!" my Teacher said.

"In Fifth Grade?" the Nurse said. "That's kind of early, don't you think?"

"Try to forgive her," my Teacher said.

"She'll have to wait till she's in Sixth!" the Nurse said.

"That's Bullshit!" my Teacher said.

"Go fight City Hall!" the Nurse said.

I would like to of seen that Film. I love Walt Disney.

But getting my Period in School like that and being only in Fifth Grade made me kind of a Heroine, if you know what I mean. The next day me and some girls had this big discussion about it before School. And the general feeling was that girls had a lot more Inconveniences happen to them than boys.

"It's not *fair*!" this one girl said.

But then this other girl said that she had a brother and she happened to know that boys got something worse than a Period except they got it in the middle of the night. It was *like* a Period this girl said, only it was called a Wet Dream and her Mother was forever having to change her brother's sheets. And this girl said that her Mother said if her brother didn't stop, they weren't going to have any sheets left to sleep on and on top of that the whole thing was a very disgusting business.

Naturally that made us feel better about Periods.

To tell the truth the Nurse in Einstein Junior High wasn't much better. You could of been dying of the Plague or something and had to crawl into her Office on your hands and knees and she always did the same thing regardless of your Medical Complaint. First she took her cigarette out of her mouth (she also smoked Marlboro but not Lights), then she took your Temperature, and then she made you drink a glass of warm water and sit on the john and count to 500 which frankly never sounded to me like very Professional Treatment. She said she wasn't allowed to Dispense Medication but if you ask me she was afraid of a Malpractice Suit which was going around among Doctors and still is, so I suppose the same thing applied to School Nurses.

Once when I didn't want to go to Gym (which I never wanted to go to and I'll tell you why later) I explained to the Nurse that I got my Period and could I be excused from Gym. Getting your Period was usually a good reason for not going to a Class, especially Gym. I guess the News of me and my Period had spread to Junior High so the Nurse let me lie down in this room that had skinny beds in it and paper on the beds which crackled whenever you moved. The door to the room was open a little bit and I heard this boy come in. I could tell by the way he talked that his nose was bleeding.

"What happened?" the Nurse said.

"My nose is bleeding," the boy said.

"I can see that," the Nurse said. "Get over here and quit dripping blood on the floor. Were you in a fight?"

"No," the boy said.

"Then why is your nose bleeding?" the Nurse said. "I have to make out a Report if you were in a fight. Were you in a fight?"

"No," the boy said.

I couldn't see them but I could picture this boy bleeding all over her floor while she made out a Report on why his nose was bleeding.

"You must of been in a fight," the Nurse said.

"I wasn't in a fight," the boy said. "Yesterday in Lacrosse Practice this kid hit me on the nose with his Lacrosse stick and I got a bloody nose and it started to bleed again. Can I lie down?"

"Are you telling me that your nose is bleeding because of something that happened *yesterday*?

Don't you know I'm not supposed to treat yesterday's Ailments today?"

That must of been News to the boy because he didn't answer her.

"Where were you yesterday?" the Nurse said.

"Where were *you*?" the boy said.

"What do you mean?" the Nurse said.

By that time I figured he was lying on his back and wouldn't be able to talk anymore.

But he said, "It happened during Lacrosse Practice after School and the Coach brought me back in the School but you had gone home already and the Coach said what good are you anyway because you leave too early and why don't you hang around when we got Lacrosse Practice. Can I lie down?"

So the Nurse told the boy to tell the Coach this place wasn't a Hospital and did he think she was on 24-hour Duty or what and the boy said he would remember that and she brought him into the little room with me. But I felt funny then with the boy lying on the other skinny bed so I told him I hoped he felt better and I went to Gym.

The Nurse gave me a dirty look when I asked for a Pass out of there but that was because she didn't like me on account of another reason. I mentioned how I was Worried about dying but it wasn't only from what Ritchie had, I also Worried about getting Tuberculosis. That's a Lung Disease which if you don't get it on your own you can get it if somebody who's got it breathes on you and you breathe in when he breathes out. I was always very careful when anybody got too close to me but sometimes they got too close when I couldn't help it so I would blow their breath away from me and try not to inhale.

I went through this Phase at the beginning of Ninth Grade where I was doing a lot of breathing out and it made me very tired. You could also *hear* me breathing out which was why my Social Studies Teacher called me The Breather and brought me down to the Nurse.

"She's breathing out," my Social Studies Teacher told her.

"I'm also breathing in," I said.

"Yeah, but you breathe out more than you breathe in. She breathes out more than she breathes in," he said.

"Does anyone in your Family have Emphysema?" the Nurse said to me.

"Maybe," I said which naturally gave me something besides Tuberculosis to think about.

The Nurse called Mom who wasn't shopping that day and Mom came up to School and took me right over to the Doctor's. The Doctor said maybe

I had an Allergy and that Mom should keep track of my breathing and if I continued to do so he would have to Take Tests.

After that I didn't breathe out in front of Teachers, only kids and strange Adults in the movies.

11

I never wanted to go to Gym for two reasons. The first was because the boys and girls in Einstein took Gym together which gave the boys their big Opportunity to make these depressing remarks concerning the condition of the girls' legs.

For instance: "Hey, Hillary! Won't your Mother let you shave yet?" (Which Hillary's Mother should of but that wasn't any of the boys' business I happened to think.)

And there was this boy Joey Falcaro who couldn't wait till I got up from the Locker Room so he could yell, "Hey, Deedie, did you get those legs off a Piano?"

These things are difficult to ignore.

But the main reason I hated Gym was because of

Mr. Campbell. Mr. Campbell was Chairman of the Phys Ed Department and he was pretty old. And because he was so old you'd think he would of known better not to do the things he did, like Touching the girls, especially me. Just because Mr. Campbell was the Head of the whole Department he seemed to think that gave him the Privilege of wandering in the Girls' Locker Room when we were dressing.

I got particularly mad one morning because I was half Naked when Mr. Campbell paraded in for his usual Bird's Eye View. Naturally he pretended he got lost and it was an Accident, but I knew it wasn't. Believe me he waited till he was all the way in the Locker Room before he said, "Whoops! Pardon me, Ladies, I must be getting Senile." Well of course we all screamed a Blue Streak and this one girl yelled, "Get outta here, you Faggot!" which should of mortified him, but no, he just stood there taking us all in, so to speak, and then he made like he was mad because we took so long getting on our Uniforms.

Now as I said I got my Period when I was only in Fifth Grade and that had a lot to do with how the rest of me was fairly Well Developed by the time of this episode. So I grabbed my shirt real quick and buttoned it up but he came right over to me with this stupid grin and he stuck his two fingers in my shirt pocket. And you know where shirt pockets are located.

"Whatcha got in there?" said Mr. Campbell.

Maybe he thought he was just Flirting but if you ask me that wasn't Flirting that was Feeling. I told Mom about it but all she said was that I had Illusions of Grandeur which meant I thought I was Hot Stuff and only imagined that Mr. Campbell was dying to know what was under my pocket. It so happened I didn't think I was Hot Stuff. I used to have an Overbite like a rabbit and even though it's better now because I wore braces I'm still inclined to be Self-Conscious about my teeth and naturally I still had that Cowlick I mentioned. So I definitely didn't think I was Hot Stuff.

Anyway Mr. Campbell was the reason I would go to the Nurse so much. But she must of kept pretty good track of my visits because she finally said: "How many times a month do you get your Period, Young Lady? I want a Note from your Doctor."

Well since she'd already sent me to the Doctor because she thought I had Emphysema I figured Mom would get a Cardiac Arrest if I had to go again. So I stopped going to the Nurse instead of Gym but from then on I made sure I got dressed very fast in the Locker Room. Mr. Campbell could have a Feel Day with somebody else for a change.

My Social Studies Teacher wasn't such a bargain either. He said very uncomplimentary things to his Students which when a Teacher says them you know if he's kidding or not. There was a girl in my Social Studies Class who was unfortunately Not Too Bright and Mr. Pendergrass, the Social Studies Teacher of whom I'm speaking, said stuff to her like, "What's the matter, Elizabeth, aren't you Playing With A Full Deck?" or "I don't think you're Wrapped Too Tight, Elizabeth," or "Didn't you take your Medication this morning, Elizabeth?" It so happened that Elizabeth did take Medication because she was Hyper and when she didn't take it she tended to act a little Dopey like she *wasn't* Playing With A Full Deck so I think it was quite unnecessary for Mr. Pendergrass to call attention to that fact.

The worst thing about Mr. Pendergrass was he liked to use Nicknames and you know how I felt about Nicknames. I already told you he called me The Breather but that was understandable because of the way I breathed when I went through my Phase. But he called other kids Nicknames because of their Physical Builds and I just didn't think that was right.

Because Mr. Pendergrass was the last person in the World who should of used Nicknames. He was extremely fat. I'm sure you must of seen those Floats they use in the Macy's Thanksgiving Day Parade. Well Mr. Pendergrass was like that. He looked like somebody stuck a hose in him and blew him up and tied his Valves just in time before he burst. And it wasn't because he had Over-Active Glands or anything, it was because he had an Over-Active Appetite. The other Teachers said they took their Life in their hands when they sat next to him in the Lunchroom, he was like a vacuum cleaner.

Well would you believe that Mr. Pendergrass had the nerve to call this boy in our Class Tons o' Fun! The thing was this boy did weigh a Ton which was all the more reason Mr. Pendergrass should of ignored his Condition because Mr. Pendergrass weighed two Tons himself and no fun about him. Frankly I think Teachers should have to take a Special Course to make them remember everything that happened to them while they were Growing Up and that Course should be number one in the Curriculum before a person can become a Teacher. When I'm a Writer (w. and i.) I'm going to write some excellent Articles on the subject. I'm just lucky I wasn't in Mr. Pendergrass's Class when I went through my Fat Period or he would of given me a Nickname too. As it was I almost got a Nickname without his help.

I was in Third Grade then. I told you how Mom was Worried about my Health after Ritchie died and she decided to fatten me up. Well she made me eat Tapioca Pudding which has all these lumps in it like something didn't dissolve, and she gave me Junket which has no lumps at all and slides down your throat so fast you think you swallowed your tongue. She also gave me very green Liver and very red Steak which was supposed to replace the blood they syphoned off at the Lab every month, and Beef Tea and Creamed Spinach and two doses of Cod Liver Oil every morning.

And these little tidbits were topped off with Calcium Tablets you could of played Backgammon with.

But the Fat Diet worked and that's how come I almost got a Nickname. I gained twenty pounds in eight weeks and Mom had to buy me all new clothes which under the circumstances was very embarrassing. Especially in A&S where the Salesgirls are quite particular who they wait on.

"Can you help us?" Mom asked the Salesgirl.

"Not in *this* Department!" said the Salesgirl and she looked at me like I was ruining the Decor of A&S which I was.

But one morning on the way to School this boy yelled out to me: "Hey, Lard Ass, you put a crack in the sidewalk!"

Which was the Nickname I almost got. Naturally I beat the Hell out of him which wasn't hard because I had all that Weight behind me. And after that I made sure to lose Mom's lunches, and at night I pushed the food around on my plate so it looked like I ate more than I did. That and getting Puberty helped a lot.

So you can see why I don't like Nicknames and how come I didn't like my Social Studies Teacher either.

Lard Ass Pendergrass in case you forgot his name.

I don't want you to think I'm a totally Negative person. I mean from what I've said so far it probably sounds like I didn't like any Teachers but that's not true. It's just that the ones I told you about didn't know how to handle kids and would of been better off in some other line of Business like Selling Insurance maybe or working for the FBI. If a person isn't happy in his Work he's more inclined to have a Mental Breakdown and it's Common Knowledge that Teachers head the list. But before I tell you about the Teachers I liked I'll fill you in on the other not-so-good ones I had in Ninth Grade.

There was Mr. Albanese who was on duty in the Cafeteria. Actually he used to be an English Teacher but there weren't enough Students to go around to give him a Class anymore. The School Board thought enrollment went down but personally I don't think it did, it only looked that way because so many kids Cut Out every day. General Wainwright High School is right next door to Einstein Junior High and at least a hundred kids would meet in the parking lot between the Schools which was where they got their weekly Supply of Grass. Naturally there were too many Business Transactions in Progress for anyone to have time to go to Class. Sometimes the kids Partied behind the Teachers' cars if the wind wasn't too strong.

Anyway Mr. Albanese became sort of a Floating Substitute. One day he'd be in the Library, another day he'd be a Math Teacher, maybe another day he'd help out in the Attendance Office. The only job they never gave him was Custodian because you have to belong to a special Union for that. He was usually in the Cafeteria though, because the other Teachers considered that Combat Duty and would of given up their Tenure to get out of it. So Mr. Albanese took that over for them which gave them the Opportunity to snag the kids who were smoking in the Bathrooms.

He had a very pleasing Personality and the only reason I'm saying he wasn't a good Teacher was that nothing bothered him. He said he would be Goddamned if he would let the kids get to him just because the Goddamned School Board made him a Goddamned baby sitter. He even used to participate in the Food Fights which he organized every Lunch Period. He always took the losing side, but even so, he was a little too lenient I thought.

I had Miss Jaborowski for Science. She wasn't a Miss because she was young, she just wasn't married yet which was probably why she was an Alcoholic. Nobody ever went up to her desk to ask a question because you got High standing next to her. Sometimes she walked around the room and looked over your shoulder which I for one found very Painful. I didn't want to Exhale like I did in my Breathing-Out Phase because she might of thought I had Emphysema and brought me down to the Nurse again. So I would hold my breath and not let the air go one way or the other.

Besides I wouldn't of hurt Miss Jaborowski for anything. She always said nice things to me like, "Deedie, Deedie, Dear ol' Deedie," and once she sang *When Johnny Comes Marching Home Again*

Hurrah Hurrah clear through to a Rousing Finish which was when she burst out crying. That's how we knew she'd had Southern Comfort in her Corn Flakes again. She was very Musical but I didn't learn much Science.

Mr. Harkavy was my Health Teacher, the one who looked up my Records. He'd had some kind of Coronary Operation which was maybe why he was a little jumpy but when I got to know him better I found him to be very friendly. He had a good heart even though it was a Pacemaker. His only trouble was that he was very puny and he was afraid of the boys because they threatened to throw him out the window if he gave Homework so he didn't give Homework.

Mrs. Vail taught Homemaking and Flirted with the Ninth Grade boys because she was getting old.

Mr. Wicks, my Study Hall Teacher, Flirted with the Ninth Grade boys for other reasons. Once in a while he Flirted with a tall Eighth Grade boy. Seventh Grade boys were out of the question.

My Music Teacher was Mrs. Cooper and all she talked about was her Grandson and she was always showing us his latest snapshots which got very boring. I mean there were just so many times you could say how cute a kid was when you really thought he had an oversize head and ears that stuck out like airplane wings.

Besides English which I'm saving for later there was one more Teacher and that was Mrs. Westfall who taught Art. Everybody called her Fuzzy-Wuzzy because she had these very hairy legs and she never shaved not even in the summer. The reason I didn't think she was a good Art Teacher was because she never gave you any Art Supplies to work with. If you needed anything for a Project you practically had to fill out an Income Tax Return to get it out of her. That's why some kids stole from her, it was like a Challenge. There was this one boy Frankie Scheulen who stole Sparkles and also some glue out of her closet. Then he went into the Boys' Room and put the glue on the Toilet Seats and then sprinkled the Sparkles over the glue. I never saw them but Allie did and she said those Toilet Seats were a Work of Art. She said it was like the King Tut Exhibit, there were so many people admiring Frankie's work. Even the Principal and the Teachers went in there. Mr. Albanese said if he would of known about it he would of sold tickets except he was stuck in the Cafeteria.

The only reason Frankie got caught was because

when he found out he created such a Stir he wanted everybody to know he did it so he went back and carved his initials underneath.

Anyway those were the Teachers on the Minus side in my opinion. Don't get me wrong, they had excellent Qualifications.

I just happened to think they were rotten Teachers.

12

The two Teachers I liked best (until Ninth Grade English) were in Elementary School.

I had Miss Offencrantz in Second Grade which was the year Ritchie died. Maybe that was why she was extra nice to me, I don't know, but I think it was just because she happened to be an extra nice person.

We used to have Show and Tell in her Class which was when you brought something from home and told everybody about it. Sometimes you didn't bring anything and in that case you only Told instead of Showed.

One day a boy got up and said he had something to Tell and not Show and you could just see how Chock Full of News he was the way he kept hopping from one foot to the other.

"Go ahead, Dear," Miss Offencrantz said.

"My dog Got Laid and had Kittens," this boy said.

Naturally nobody knew what Getting Laid meant (except Miss Offencrantz) but you could tell by her face she was kind of impressed. Then she giggled and said: "You mean Puppies, Dear, not Kittens."

Later on of course I knew what Getting Laid was but you can see what a good Teacher Miss Offencrantz was not to correct that boy except to say it was Puppies and not Kittens.

The other reason I liked her was this. It was about a week after that boy's dog had Puppies and I said I had something to Tell and not Show and I asked her if that would be all right.

"Do you have any Pets?" Miss Offencrantz said.

"No," I said.

"Good," Miss Offencrantz said. "Go ahead, Deedie."

Well I don't remember where I heard it but somebody once told me that if you put salt in the palm of your hand you could catch a bird. So I told my Class and Miss Offencrantz that the day before I'd gone out in my backyard with salt in the palm of my hand and I caught a bird just that way. I may of mentioned that I have a very good Imagination and when I told that story I told it quite well with a lot of Details and I even convinced myself that it was true. But when the kids in my Class asked me where the bird was because naturally they didn't believe me, Miss Offencrantz said, "Why, Deedie let the little bird go back to its nest, didn't you, Deedie?"

So I said, "Why yes, I let the little bird go back to its nest."

Then Miss Offencrantz said it was very kind of me to let that little bird go back to its nest or it would of been terribly scared if I'd brought it to School where it couldn't fly around.

After I got out of Second Grade I used to see Miss Offencrantz in the hall now and then and she never said Boo about the bird, she just smiled at me in her nice way and said, "Hello, Deedie, and how are you this Fine Morning?"

But one day I don't know how come it hit me, maybe I jumped up a couple of spurts in Maturity or something, I suddenly realized that Miss Offencrantz knew I hadn't caught a bird in my hand at all. So I went back to her Classroom to tell her what a good Teacher she was but there was another Teacher in that room.

"I'm sorry," said this other Teacher. "Miss Offencrantz moved to Buffalo over the Summer and she's Mrs. Reif now. Didn't you know she got Married and moved away?"

"No," I said.

I've thought a lot about Miss Offencrantz (I mean Mrs. Reif) since then. And I feel a little sad that I never got to tell her how Wonderful I thought she was. And I wonder if she had a baby yet and if she did, I guess by now that baby is in School already and Miss Offencrantz (Mrs. Reif) has forgotten me by now. But even if she has ten children, which she should, and every one of them tells her they caught a bird by putting salt in their hands I'll bet she'll make like she believes them because she's just that kind of person.

Her children must love her very much. I know I do.

My other favorite Teacher was Mr. Oliver in Fifth Grade. He was a brand-new Teacher and he hadn't had time yet to develop any negative feelings about kids. Don't ask me why but once I told Mr. Oliver that my Family was on Welfare and that Mom was too proud to use Food Stamps. We'd been talking about Poor People that day and when the bell rang I kind of hung around in the room till I was the last one there and the words just came out.

The next day Mr. Oliver called me up to his desk at the end of the day and handed me this brown Grocery bag. I looked inside and there was a giant-size loaf of Wonder Bread in the bag.

"What's this for?" I said.

Mr. Oliver got real embarrassed and his face got very red and he coughed a lot like Teachers do when they don't know what to say. Finally he told me, "Just bring it home, Deedie, and let's say no more about it, all right? See if you can get it into the house without your Parents seeing it."

Then he patted me on the head and gave me this big wink like we had a Wonderful Secret between us which we now did.

Well naturally I knew right away he thought we were too poor to buy Wonder Bread and I should of straightened that out but he looked so pleased with himself that I didn't have the Heart to say anything except Thank You. I could of thrown the Bread away on the way home from School or at least given it to a Poor Person but I didn't know any.

"Who bought the Wonder Bread?" said Mom that night.

"Oh," I said like I forgot all about that Wonder Bread. "Mr. Oliver shopped on his Lunch Hour and he bought an extra loaf of Wonder Bread so he gave me one."

A couple of days later Mr. Oliver gave me another brown Grocery bag with a dozen eggs in it.

"Where did the dozen eggs come from?" Mom said.

"Mr. Oliver overshopped again," I said. "And his wife is getting mad because he's wasting their money." I was beginning to put in Details and that Worried me but I couldn't help myself.

Three days later I got another loaf of Wonder Bread and a jar of Peanut Butter which was the kind I happened to like because it had chunks of peanuts in it.

"I don't understand," Mom said.

"I won the Spelling Bee," I said.

"That's a peculiar prize," Mom said.

"I know," I said because it was.

The two quarts of Milk were for Perfect Attendance for a week. The four Lamb chops were because I was the only Student who didn't copy on a Test. (Which was true but I was also the only Student who didn't *pass* the Test.) The Swiss Cheese was because Mr. Oliver was Allergic to Swiss Cheese and the American Cheese was because *Mrs.* Oliver was Allergic to American Cheese.

After one pound of butter, three Pork roasts, enough fresh vegetables to make six salads, and one pair of Winter gloves Mrs. Oliver outgrew I ran out of excuses.

So I told Mr. Oliver that my Uncle Henry died After A Long Illness and left us a lot of money. He'd been a Recluse in the city, I said, and nobody knew he would die a Wealthy Man.

Mr. Oliver looked at me for a long time.

Finally he said, "You're not on Welfare anymore?"

"No," I said which of course was true.

He looked at me for another long time and I could tell he was thinking about the two loaves of Wonder Bread, the dozen eggs, the jar of the kind of Peanut Butter I like because it has chunks of peanuts in it, the two quarts of Milk, the four Lamb chops, the Swiss Cheese, the American Cheese, the one pound of butter, the three Pork roasts, the fresh vegetables that were enough to make six salads, and the one pair of Winter gloves Mrs. Oliver outgrew.

"He died a Wealthy Man?" Mr. Oliver said.

"Yes," I said.

"And you're very rich now," Mr. Oliver said.

"Yes," I said. "But don't congratulate my Mother. She doesn't want anybody to know."

"Why not?" Mr. Oliver said.

"She's afraid I'll get Kidnaped," I said.

"Right-o!" Mr. Oliver said.

He hardly talked to me for the rest of the year. Once near the end of Fifth Grade he said he liked the skirt I was wearing and he asked me where I got it.

"A&S," I said and he said, "Mm," and patted me on the head again.

But he never called Mom and he never brought up the subject of the Groceries. The last day of School he said, "Take care, Kid, don't take any Wooden Nickels," and I said, "You neither, Mr. Oliver," and that was the end of the Discussion.

But I used to wonder if Mr. Oliver and Miss Offencrantz who is now Mrs. Reif ever talked about me.

I hope not.

13

I think there's a difference between lying and Exercising Your Imagination. I mean I know those stories I told were lies but I don't think they showed any particular Criminal Tendencies on my part. Outside of taking some Wrigley Spearmint from the 7 Eleven without paying, the only really Criminal Act I performed was to steal my best friend's Four-Color Ball-Point pen.

Mom thought I told stories just to call attention to myself but that wasn't true. If there was one thing I had, it was attention after Ritchie died. Because all of a sudden I was An Only Child. If you're An Only Child all along you get used to it, but when you become one like I did I think it's a different kind of Situation. So I'm not bragging when I say I have a good Imagination. It was born out of necessity, you might say, when I had nobody to talk to.

Which is why I like big Families. In big Families there's always somebody to keep a conversation going if a couple of members aren't talking to each other. There aren't any Lulls. But in my house when Mom wasn't talking to Daddy there was nobody but me to stop the Lulls.

That's why I said my Imagination came from necessity. I mean I had to jabber away at the dinner table just to get Mom talking to Daddy again, and if I had nothing to tell I used to make things up. It was during one of those Lulls that I gave myself a sister. That is I *pretended* to give myself a sister and I named her Eleanor. She was nine years old like me.

Mom got real Worried when I told her about Eleanor.

"What do you mean you have a sister?" Mom said.

"She's a *pretend* sister," I said.

"Why?" Mom said.

"Because I like her," I said.

"Are you looking for attention?" Mom said.

"No," I said.

"Then why pretend you have a sister?" Mom said.

"I like to talk to her," I said.

"Why don't you talk to me?" Mom said.

"I *am* talking to you," I said and I was.

"Stop talking and eat your dinner," Mom said.

Of course Mom told Uncle Freddie and Aunt Nina about Eleanor. She even told the Doctor who helped fatten me up that time. They all said there was nothing wrong with me having a pretend sister but Mom Worried anyhow. Once I heard the Doctor tell her: "It's Only Natural Under the Circumstances," which Mom must of repeated to the whole Family, because then they asked all these questions to show me how Normal I was.

"Hi, Deedie," Aunt Nina would say. "How's Eleanor?"

And Uncle Freddie once called and said, "What's new with Eleanor, Deedie? Hey, how's she getting along in School?"

If you want to know it sounded like he wanted me to call Eleanor to the phone so she could tell him herself, that's how ridiculous it got. I mean they were trying to show me they didn't think I was crazy so they asked me about somebody who didn't exist which made me think *they* were crazy.

So I'd say, "She's okay I guess," or "Oh, yeah, Eleanor likes School a lot."

Nobody understood that Eleanor wasn't someone I wanted to share. She was just for me.

Except Daddy. Mom was giving me the Third

Degree once and Daddy said, "Well *I* like Eleanor. She sounds like a good kid, if you ask me," which of course Mom didn't and we had another one of those Lulls I told you about.

Eleanor didn't last very long. One day Mom heard me talking in my room and she opened my door. Actually the funny thing was I wasn't talking to Eleanor, I was talking to my mirror, pretending I was a Famous Writer getting interviewed by Dick Cavett.

"Who are you talking to?" Mom said.

To tell the truth I was getting tired of the whole business of Eleanor and I wanted to get rid of her anyway. So instead of telling Mom I was discussing my Career with Dick Cavett I said, "Only Eleanor."

Ordinarily Mom wasn't a hollerer. Especially after Ritchie died, she hardly did any hollering at all. But even when Mom was mad-*soft,* you could tell there was a lot more inside her that she wanted to come out and wouldn't let it.

Except this time the You-Know-What Hit The Fan. Mom screamed that I should Stop This Nonsense and why did I take such a Supreme Delight in Making Her Miserable and a whole lot of other stuff and then all of a sudden she said: "This is the *end* of Eleanor! Eleanor just died! *Today we bury Eleanor!*"

Well that scared me so much I couldn't talk. Because Eleanor's dying made me think of Ritchie and I suddenly wondered if Ritchie had to die just to get away from Mom. I got a little mad too and I wanted to ask Mom if I was really her Two-In-One how come she didn't love me twice as much now that Ritchie wasn't here.

I didn't say anything though and now that I'm older I'm glad I didn't. I mean now that I think about it, maybe I *made* myself a little strange just to scare Mom. Maybe I did take a Supreme Delight in Making Her Miserable so she'd notice me more and stop thinking about Ritchie.

Ritchie was very smart in School but maybe he wouldn't of been if I'd died instead of him. Plenty of times I used to wish it was the other way around, then Ritchie would have to write Poems for Mom instead of bringing her the Geraniums he wanted to. And maybe he would of been the one to take a Sup. Delight in Making Her Miserable because Mom would be missing me and not him. I guess that was the main reason I wished Ritchie didn't die which was kind of selfish of me and I'm ashamed of that now, but don't forget I was only nine years old at the time.

Anyway I never mentioned Eleanor again. But Mom used to tell that story to everyone because she thought it was funny. She still tells it once in a while, how cleverly she got rid of my pretend sister.

"I just told Deedie that Eleanor died and that was the end of Eleanor," she says, and then she laughs and hugs me like I think it's funny too.

Once when we were alone Daddy told me he hoped Eleanor was happy where she was but I didn't say anything. I didn't want him to cry in the night like he did over Ritchie. Because I just knew Daddy missed Eleanor as much as I did. I don't think that anymore but I think Mom could of found a better way to get rid of Eleanor.

I mean she didn't have to kill her.

The last time I Over-Exercised my Imagination was when I told my Sixth Grade Class that Kristy McNichol was my sister. Where Eleanor had been just for me, I wanted everybody to know about Kristy.

Naturally they asked some very excellent questions.

"If she's your sister why don't you live with her in California?" and "When is she coming home for a visit?" and "How come her last name is McNichol and your last name is Wooster?" and "Yeah, hey, how come she doesn't have the same last name as you?"

So I said that first of all she had to change her name to McNichol because who ever heard of a big TV Star named Wooster? And I said that second of all since she was such a big TV Star, naturally she couldn't get away from her Studio because her Program was always In Production and how was she supposed to commute from California to Long Island even though she would of preferred to be with her Family who she loved and missed very much.

"But she calls us from California at least two or three times a week," I said.

That was a mistake because then my Sixth Grade Class wanted to be at my house when Kristy called so I said the Time Zone was crazy in California and we had to talk to her in the middle of the night and did they think their Parents would let them come over my house in the middle of the night and of course their Parents wouldn't which I had hoped.

Then one girl said I should have a Pajama Party because that way there would be an excuse for everybody to be there when Kristy called but I said Mom wouldn't let the boys be at our Pajama Party and it wouldn't be fair for just the girls to talk to Kristy and not the boys even though the boys didn't express any desire to talk to her.

What the boys did express was that I should

prove some other way that Kristy McNichol was my sister. So I bought a picture of Kristy McNichol in a Poster store and on the picture I wrote myself a little message from Kristy:

> To my darling sister Deedie who I miss very much because I have to live in California on account of my Program is always In Production.
>
> Love, your VERY BUSY sister Kristy.

That quieted my Sixth Grade Class down for a while, even the boys. But then, like I did with the other stories, I added more Details. I said that Kristy was coming home for Christmas. I figured that was pretty safe because nobody ever came over to my house anyway.

They called though. Every hour on the hour the phone rang and it was an interested member of my Sixth Grade Class wanting to talk to Kristy. I was afraid to move away from the phone even to go to the Bathroom.

"Who's calling you so much?" Mom said.

"Friends," I said.

"How come you have so many friends all of a sudden?" Mom said.

"I got Popular all of a sudden," I said.

Mom was always wishing I got Popular so I

knew that would satisfy her. But one day she said, "Deedie, we need Potatoes. Please go to the store."

"I'm expecting a Call," I said.

"I'll take the Message," Mom said.

"Don't answer it," I said. "They'll call back."

But I'll tell you, I was getting as sick of the Kristy McNichol business as I got of Eleanor so I took my time going to the store and I took my time coming back and even then I didn't go into the house. I went in my backyard with the Potatoes and kind of fooled around doing this and that before I went in.

Sure enough Mom had this funny look on her face when I gave her the Potatoes.

"Who's Chrissy?" Mom said.

"Who?" I said.

"I think that's who they wanted," Mom said. "It sounded like Chrissy."

"Kristy you mean?" I said.

"Christy then," Mom said. "Who's Christy?"

"*I* don't know," I said. "Why?"

"Because the phone rang a million times and your friends wanted a Chrissy or a Christy Somebody or other," Mom said.

"*I* don't know," I said.

"But who is she?" Mom said.

"It could of been a Wrong Number," I said.

"A million Wrong Numbers?" Mom said.

"*I* don't know," I said.

"How could you not know?" Mom said. "You knew they wanted a Christy and not a Chrissy. So how could you not know?"

"*I* don't know," I said.

You could see I put myself in a Desperate Situation on purpose. So after Christmas I told my Sixth Grade Class that Kristy didn't come home because she was In Production again and now Mom was mad because it just showed that even when your own child or sister became a big TV Star she could get very Stuck Up and now we didn't want to hear from her no matter what so there was no reason for them to call my house anymore.

I wrote to Kristy McNichol last year to tell her that story because I thought it was funny.

So far I haven't heard from her.

14

Maybe you were surprised to hear I Shoplifted some Wrigley's Spearmint and that I stole my best friend's Four-Color Ball-Point pen, but that was chicken-feed in comparison to a lot of other kids. I know some girls who go to the local K mart store and Shoplift on a weekly basis. They don't consider a week worth mentioning unless they add twenty dollars worth of Merchandise to their wardrobes. And they don't even wait for a Sale, which if they're going to Shoplift you'd think would be the least they could do.

For instance first they pick out a goodly supply of Bras, then they go into this room in the Bra Department and put on the new Bras, then they put their old Bra on top. When they go out of that store believe me they're a lot Bustier than when they came in. The store must go crazy around Inventory Time.

I never did anything as crooked as that except for that Four-Color Ball-Point pen and I want you to know about it so you can be sure I learned my lesson. In a way it was the same sort of thing as the Kristy McNichol business and my pretend sister Eleanor because as soon as I took that pen I wanted to get rid of it.

First of all I didn't really steal it from my best friend. I mean I stole the pen and all but the girl wasn't my best friend, she was only my next door neighbor who has sinced moved away Thank Goodness. I think her Parents wanted to get her as far away from me as possible but if you want to know she was one of the girls who used to steal Bras in K mart which naturally her Parents didn't know and they thought she was an Absolute Angel. Daddy said the reason they moved was because her Father was an Engineer and was always getting transferred but I personally think Daddy was only trying to make me feel better even though he was very mad at the time. Daddy's a lot different than Mom, he can understand when a person makes a mistake. Mom is like an elephant and never forgets.

Anyway this girl Lisa hardly had any friends because her Family moved around so much so our Mothers thought it would be nice if we exchanged Christmas Presents. Actually our Mothers bought the Presents with their own money so it didn't cost me and Lisa a cent.

So I brought my Present over to Lisa on Christmas Day and she gave me her Present and then she took me into her room to show me what else she got, including the latest Bra she ripped off from Mays. While she was putting it back in her drawer so her Mother wouldn't see it I saw this interesting-looking pen on her desk.

"Did you get this pen for Christmas?" I said.

"Yes," Lisa said. "It's a Four-Color Ball-Point pen."

"How does it work?" I said.

Lisa showed me and let me tell you I thought it was just fantastic. I mean I never saw a pen like that in my entire Life. It wasn't like other pens that only had one point, instead it had four little buttons that you could push up and down to get a different color ink. Naturally I wanted a Four-Color Ball-Point pen like that because you can see how handy it was.

So when Lisa wasn't looking I put it in my pocket.

She showed me the rest of her Presents and then

she said, "Let's go back in the Living Room. I want to show you what I bought my Parents."

Now this is the part where you could see how much I wanted to get rid of that pen. Because I said, "Why don't you put all your things away so they don't get lost?"

"I'll put them away later," Lisa said. "I want to show you what I bought my Parents."

"No," I said. "Put them away now. Especially your Four-Color Ball-Point pen. Where is it?"

"It's on the desk," Lisa said. "Let's—"

"No it isn't," I said.

Well naturally Lisa started hunting high and low for her Four-Color Ball-Point pen which was nowhere to be seen because it was now in my pocket.

"It's got to be here in the room," Lisa said, "because didn't I just show it to you?"

"Yes," I said, "so we better keep looking."

Finally Lisa called her brother Norman in the room to help us look. I really hated her brother Norman because he once set fire to our fence which Mom said was Understandable Under the Circumstances since Norman didn't have any friends because his Family moved around so much and he was Looking for Attention. Mom always understood why other kids did things.

Anyway Norman came in and then the three of us started looking for that Four-Color Ball-Point pen which I don't have to tell you we couldn't find.

Then I said: "I'll look under the bed. If it fell on the floor it would of rolled under the bed."

And while I was on my knees looking under Lisa's bed all of a sudden Norman let out this yell.

"*There's* your pen! In Deedie's back pocket! You Friggin' Crook, you! Give my sister back her pen!"

So Lisa started to cry and I started to cry and of course Lisa's Parents came running into the room to see what was all the Hullabaloo. When they found out what I did they chased me out and told me never to come back and they were going to call my Parents which they did.

As I walked across the yard I could still hear them giving Lisa the Absolute Angel the Benefit of their Advice.

"You are never to play with that child again!" Lisa's Mother said. "She's a Bad Influence!"

"I don't want her in this house, do you hear?" Lisa's Father said.

"I *knew* she was a Friggin' Crook!" Norman said and they didn't even tell him to watch his language.

I was Grounded for two weeks which was no Big Deal since I never went anyplace. Daddy never mentioned the Incident again but for a long time after that Mom looked at me kind of funny when she couldn't find anything.

Lisa's Family moved away a month later. I don't know where they went because they didn't keep in touch.

15

Till I met Allie in Junior High, Lisa was the closest I got to having a best friend. I think I already explained I was no Raving Beauty so the boys didn't flock around me and because the boys didn't flock around neither did the girls. Girls flock where boys flock if you know what I mean. And since I didn't sell Grass because even if I would of wanted to I wouldn't of known where to buy it to sell it, that eliminated the other half of the School. You could say Deedie Wooster was not in Public Demand.

But I almost got Popular because I belonged to a Club once. Except that I only belonged to that Club for exactly one day so I'll never know how Popular I would of been if I'd lasted. I wish I could say I quit but I didn't. I got kicked out.

First of all I want to say I never thought much of Clubs. It seemed to me the only reason kids organized a Club was because they had a friend they were mad at and they wanted to show that friend how mad they were so they organized a Club and asked everybody to join except the friend they were mad at. Which was what happened to me in the Eighth Grade.

I was in the Cafeteria eating my Lunch by myself because Allie was absent. All of a sudden a bunch of girls sat down at my table. None of them looked at me when they sat down and if you want to know I don't think they even knew I was there till this one girl spilled her soup in my lap. It wasn't on purpose or anything and if it hadn't landed on me I might of thought it was funny the way that soup just slid off her tray right into my lap. Of course she said she was sorry and I could see she really was because she ran to get some napkins to mop up the soup. Then she made her friends help her pick off all the vegetables that stuck to me and I must say they were all very sociable about it.

"What's your name?" one of the girls said.

"Deedie Wooster," I said.

"Oh," she said, kind of unimpressed because between you and me my name didn't mean anything to her. It wasn't like I was Class President, if you know what I mean. Then they all sat down again and let me listen while they made these plans for the Club they happened to be organizing at the time.

The girl whose soup slid into my lap, whose name I found out was Kathy, said, "But we can't be The Sexy Six if there's only five of us, Doreen. How can we be The Sexy Six with only five girls?"

And Doreen said, "Then we'll pick another name. Think of another name, Kathy."

And Kathy said, "I can't, can you?"

"No," Doreen said.

"Besides," said another girl whose name I never found out, "*Mindy* knows we want to be The Sexy Six and if we only get five girls then she'll be glad."

"Yeah," said two other girls whose names I also never found out.

"Yeah," Doreen and Kathy said.

Then Doreen said, "So why don't we pick someone else to be in the Club and make sure *Mindy* finds out and *boy* will she be mad, okay?"

And Kathy said, "*Yeah!* Mindy'll be so mad she'll just drop dead she'll be so mad! What do you think, everybody?"

Well naturally Doreen said it was a good idea since she thought of it in the first place and then the other three girls whose names I never found out also agreed it would be good if Mindy dropped dead and all of a sudden they looked at me.

"You want to be in our Club?" said Kathy who was obviously going to be the President. "It's called The Sexy Six."

"Sure," I said.

"What's your name again?" Kathy said.

"Deedie Wooster," I said.

"Okay, Deedie," Kathy said. "Well have our first meeting on Friday at my house at ten in the morning. My Mother goes to work around nine. Is ten o'clock okay for everybody?"

"Yeah," everybody said.

"Don't we have School on Friday?" I said.

They all looked at me kind of funny, then they started to laugh. "Are you kidding, Deedie?" Kathy said. "Of course we have School Friday. We're just not going, that's all."

"Oh," I said.

"Okay," Kathy said. "That's settled. Now, we ha—"

"Why can't we have the meeting after School?" I said. "Or Friday *night* maybe." Friday nights I only watched TV anyway.

"And not hang out at Hero-Burger?" Doreen said. "We hang out at Hero-Burger Friday night."

"Oh," I said. Now I didn't know if The Sexy

Six hung out in front of Hero-Burger, the sides of Hero-Burger, or the *back* of Hero-Burger, and to tell the truth I didn't want to ask. I mean I was so glad they wanted me in their Club I didn't want to louse it up with too many questions. I figured I'd find out Friday night, if Mom let me out that is.

But the ten o'clock business Worried me. I'd never Cut School in my entire Life and I didn't know the first way to go about it. Like did I bring a Note to Attendance on Monday or what? And who would sign it? A couple of times I'd written a Note for Allie and signed it like she told me but it sort of scared me to do it for myself. I would of asked Allie to do it except I didn't want her to feel bad that I was asked to join The Sexy Six and she wasn't.

But I remembered how Mom was always saying I should come to her when I had a Problem so that's what I did. I just didn't tell her what the Problem was exactly. Now I'm really ashamed to tell you this because you'll say it was dumb of me and as it turned out you'd be absolutely right but dumb or not I asked Mom.

"Could you write me a Note because I have to stay home from School on Friday?" I said.

"Why?" Mom said. "What's Friday?"

"I have to stay home from School," I said.

"Do we have a Doctor's appointment?" Mom said.

"No," I said.

"So what's Friday?" Mom said.

"I have a Club Meeting," I said.

"What Club?" Mom said. "You belong to a Club?"

"Yes," I said.

"You didn't tell me you belonged to a Club," Mom said. "What Club?"

Well if we were called The Science Club or The Ecology Club or The Environmental Club or The Creative Writing Club I would of told her that, but I certainly didn't want to say we were The Sexy Six Club. And while I was thinking what to tell Mom was the name of our Club, she also thought up a lot more questions to ask me. It turned out I finally told her about how these girls sat down at the Cafeteria table with me and how Kathy spilled her soup in my lap and how they were very sociable and let me in their Club and that the first meeting was Friday morning at ten o'clock.

"Who are the girls?" Mom said.

So I told her about Kathy and Doreen and the other three girls whose names I didn't know.

"But not Mindy," I said.

"Who's Mindy?" Mom said.

"I don't know," I said, "but she's not in the Club."

By that time I figured I wasn't either so I told Mom to forget the whole thing, I would go to School on Friday.

But Mom didn't forget the whole thing, she called the School the next morning and told them the plans of The Sexy Six. And as soon as Homeroom started a Messenger came up from Mr. Kramer the Assistant Principal and I had to go down to his Office. Let me tell you I was scared because you only went to Mr. Kramer's Office when you Cut School or even one Class which I never did either.

Well Mr. Kramer was like the CIA and he got all this information out of me about the Club I didn't belong to anymore and the names of the girls which I said were Kathy and Doreen and three more girls whose names I didn't know.

"Oh, yeah," Mr. Kramer said, "The Einstein Irregulars," like he knew them very well. Then he thanked me for my excellent Cooperation and told me to go back to Homeroom.

"Those girls are bad news, Deedie," Mr. Kramer said. "Stay away from them."

Which wasn't necessary for him to tell me because I tried to stay as far away from them as possible. But every time they saw me in the halls they called me a Rat Fink and then pretty soon the whole School was calling me a Rat Fink. Allie and Dennis were the only ones who talked to me during that time (except for Mr. Kramer). Of course I'm sure Heather would of if she'd been there but she was up in Nova Scotia she told me after she came back. And Allie was very understanding when I told her why I didn't ask her to write an Absence Note for me.

"Shit, Deedie," Allie said. "I wouldn't of felt bad not being in their stupid Club. They're all Tramps anyway and they hang out in back of Hero-Burger every Friday night. I see them all the time."

I found out later that they let Mindy in The Sexy Six Club anyway and they even let her be the President to show they weren't mad anymore. The rest of the School stopped calling me Rat Fink after a while except for Doreen and Kathy and Mindy.

And the other three girls whose names I never found out.

16

But I wished I hadn't been kicked out of that Club for one reason. At least I would of had a boyfriend which every one of those girls did. Occasionally they changed boyfriends but it was mostly with each other and even though somebody was always crying because her boyfriend Broke Up with her to go with somebody else in the Club, by the end of Eighth Period they all had a boyfriend again if only Temporarily.

Frankly I like boys and always did. I don't know if boys liked me though because none of them ever said anything to me about it. But in Third Grade I really liked this boy whose name was Gerald Marks.

From the very first day of School that year I wished with all my heart I could sit next to him but he was very short and as I said I was always sat in the back because of my Height. It didn't matter though, because from the back of the room I could keep my eyes on Gerald Marks all day which I did. And all day I Observed how Gerald Marks teased this girl who sat in the next row to him.

He would punch her in the arm or slam her book shut or throw spitballs at her or write on her desk or poke her in the leg with the wire on his Spiral Notebook which always stuck out after a couple of days, which he did because naturally that was how boys of that Age show a girl how much they like her. So more than anything I wanted Gerald Marks to punch me in the arm or slam my book shut or even just poke me in the leg with the wire from his Spiral Notebook. I would of even been satisfied if he only chased me around the room like he sometimes did with that girl.

But he didn't. So I started to punch him in the arm whenever I passed his desk but he still wouldn't pay attention to me. Finally I figured I would hit him and run away so he'd chase me around the room and I could scream like the other girl did.

Well I hit Gerald Marks but I must of given him such a shot that he started to cry. Then he began to scream just like that girl screamed and he ran away from me clear to the other side of the room.

Naturally I thought he wanted me to chase *him*, but when I caught up with him he said if I didn't leave him alone he would tell his Mother. I was very embarrassed by that, especially since he now had this mark on his arm like I hit him with a baseball bat. I decided right then and there I didn't like him anymore. I never found out if he liked me either.

When I got a little higher in Elementary School, Mom began to tell me all these stories about how men liked to Play With Little Girls and I should never go with a strange man or a strange woman either because sometimes strange women liked to do the same things strange men did except in a different way. Which I didn't understand at the time and to tell the truth I still don't even though I hear about stuff like that from time to time.

Mom's stories got a lot worse when I got to Junior High, because then she told me I didn't only have to Worry about strange men and women but now I had to worry about boys my own Age and how they could get a girl Pregnant if the girl didn't understand how that worked. And even if the girl understood how it worked and didn't want to, sometimes the boy would make her.

If you want to know I didn't think any boy my own Age could get me Pregnant if I didn't want him to. I mean even in Junior High they were still shorter and skinnier than me and frankly it embarrassed me when I had to stand next to them. Of course I slouched a good deal but the difference was obvious especially on top where I looked like an Older Woman. So I wasn't afraid of boys, even Joey Falcaro who I told you called me Piano Legs. He was a head shorter than me and though I hated him he was no threat to me Sexually.

Anyway by the time I was in Seventh Grade I wasn't as Illiterate about Sex as Mom thought I was and I certainly knew how a boy could get a girl Pregnant especially after Allie'd played that trick on Heather with the Jergen's Lotion which she said was Semen. What I couldn't figure out was how the boy got his Semen into the girl without her knowing it and when I found out *how* he got it in I don't have to tell you that the possibility of any boy getting his Semen into me was pretty Farfetched. I mean it was the most disgusting thing I ever heard.

In Eighth Grade my thoughts on the subject changed a little. Because when I liked a boy in Eighth and I would think about him I'd get this funny feeling very low in my stomach. It was kind of nice and made my legs feel sort of wobbly or weak or something. It's hard to explain so I don't know if you know what I mean exactly but it was the very same feeling I got in bed at night with my pillow. I mean all of a sudden I'd find I'd put my pillow between my legs and was squeezing it tight and enjoying it very much.

I'd never told that to anybody but once Allie said she did the same thing so I told her I did it too. Allie said it was called Masturbation so I looked it up in the School Dictionary because frankly I was a little Worried about doing it. It wasn't in that Dictionary which Worried me even more. Then I looked it up in the Dictionary we have at home and I found it which made me feel better since what I was doing actually had a name. I figured that as long as it had a name it must of been a pretty common thing or else how would there be something to call it? When I was little I had the same sort of Theory about Santa Claus. Even when I was told there was no such person as Santa Claus I decided there really had to be, otherwise how could there be so many pictures of him? But every once in a while when I squeezed my pillow with my legs I'd Worry and remember there wasn't a Santa Claus so maybe there wasn't such a thing as Masturbation either and maybe I was doing something I shouldn't. I did it anyway though, because I figured if there wasn't such a thing maybe there should be which I admit is only my opinion.

But I never asked Mom about Masturbation even though she said I should come to her if I had a question about Sex. To tell the truth I don't think I could go to Mom if by Accident I ever got Pregnant and I'll tell you why. She once told me a story about something that happened to a girl she knew in High School and Mom said she'd never forget it as long as she lives and that's why a girl should always be able to come to her Mother if she gets In Trouble. "In Trouble" is Mom's way of saying Getting Pregnant Before Marriage. What happened was this.

This girl Mom knew was going with a boy and they went All The Way and the girl got Pregnant. Now when Mom was in High School there was no such thing as an Abortion. I mean there was, but you weren't allowed to get one anyplace even if you weren't Catholic. It's different now of course and I think even Catholics are allowed Abortions as long as their Priest says it's okay with him but in Mom's day nobody could, no matter if you were Protestant or Jewish or a Religion of your own making.

Well it seems this girl couldn't tell her Mother so she and her boyfriend got into his car one night and turned on the Ignition and kept the windows shut up tight and when they were found in the morning they were both deader than doornails.

"And they were only Seventeen years old, Deedie, and their Lives were over," Mom said.

"That's terrible," I said.

"Isn't that terrible?" Mom said.

"Yes, that's terrible," I said which I'd said already.

"Terrible," Mom said.

Then I didn't say anything because Mom was right and it *was* terrible and since we both agreed on that I thought the conversation was over but to my surprise it wasn't.

"You see, Deedie," Mom said, "if that poor girl could of come to her Mother when she got In Trouble she would of been alive today. Do you see that?"

"Yes," I said.

"What do you think, Darling?" Mom said.

"I think it was terrible," I said.

"No," Mom said, "I mean don't you think she should of come to her Mother when she found out she was In Trouble?"

"Or the boy's Mother even," I said.

"Why would she go to the boy's Mother?" Mom said.

"Wasn't he In Trouble too?" I said.

"The *boy*!" Mom said. "What did *he* have to lose?"

"Then why did he kill himself?" I said.

"Where *are* you, Deedie?" Mom said. "Are you being Deliberately Dense? Don't you understand what I'm talking about?"

"Yes," I said.

"Well that's what I mean," Mom said. "Would you be able to come to me if you got In Trouble?"

"Sure," I said even though I wasn't. I mean the whole conversation was beginning to sound dumb to me.

"What do you mean 'Sure'?" Mom said.

"What do you mean what do I mean?" I said.

"I mean," Mom said, "would you be able to come to me . . . if you got . . . In Trouble!"

When Mom talked slow like that the whole world could tell she was mad.

"And I said 'Sure' because I *would* be able to come to you!" I said.

"Are you telling me there's a possibility you would get In Trouble?" Mom said.

"Me?" I said.

"Because, Deedie," Mom said, "if you ever did such a thing I'd be—oh, my *God*!—I'd be so . . . so *disappointed* in you! I don't know what I'd *do*! Daddy *too,* remember!" which she said because Daddy usually wasn't as disappointed in what I did as Mom was.

"Mom!" I said. "I'd never—"

"Listen, Deedie," Mom said, "just because the whole world's gone crazy and This One is sleeping with That One, we still believe in Marriage in this

Family and if you ever told us you wanted to move in with a boy before you got Married—"

"Mom!" I said. "I'd never—"

"—I mean it would be just terrible for me!" Mom said. "*And* Daddy! And if you ever got *Pregnant,* my *God*—it would be—"

"But boys don't even *like* me!" I said.

I shouldn't of broken the News to her like that but I didn't know how else to straighten her out.

"Why not?" Mom said. "Are you too Aggressive?"

So I said I had a lot of Homework and could we talk about it another time.

But I want you to know I would never get In Trouble anyway and if I did maybe I would get an Abortion and maybe I wouldn't, I don't know. But I certainly wouldn't want to die the way Mom's friend in High School did.

Either way Mom would be disappointed in me.

17

I made another friend in Ninth Grade and to tell the truth I didn't miss Allie as much as I thought I would. For one thing she joined The Sexy Six which then became The Sexy Seven and for another thing Allie was now their new President and Kathy's best friend. Allie said she would of stayed my best friend if I could of hung out at Hero-Burger but since I couldn't she was Kathy's.

But I met this girl in my English Class named Gina Sarlo who was a lot like me. She was a very nice person and knew about as much as I did Sexually which more or less gave us something in common. She also had a cousin in Eleventh Grade who was willing to share her information with Gina who was willing to share it with me. The reason I liked Gina was because when she told me something I didn't know she never said, "Shit, Deedie, didn't you know that?" the way Allie did. Like about Soul-Kissing for instance.

Frankly Soul-Kissing disgusted me almost as much as when I found out how a boy got his Semen into you and Gina was just as disgusted as I was about both those things which shows you how alike we were. Gina said her cousin said that Soul-Kissing is the same as French Kissing and we were both surprised that people kissed differently in different Countries. And we both agreed we didn't like the way people kissed in France.

I don't know if Gina objected for the same reason I did but I'll tell you why I didn't like it. Pure and simple it just didn't appeal to me. And the other reason was, knowing me, I'd start to Worry about getting Tuberculosis and then dying all over again. I mean when you're kissing a boy you could hold your breath for a while and not inhale whatever he was breathing out just in case. But in Soul-Kissing you'd actually be taking those Germs right into your mouth which was just looking for trouble, if you ask me. And Gina's cousin said that Soul-Kissing could lead to getting Pregnant which I doubted at the time but don't anymore now that I'm older.

Anyway Gina and I became quite friendly and she invited me to my first Boy-Girl Party. Most of the kids in my School had been attending Boy-Girl Parties for a long time but that was my first. Naturally when I told Mom I was invited to a Party she wanted to know whose Party and if there were going to be boys there and if Gina's Parents were going to be home and a whole lot of other stuff that I couldn't see made any difference at a Party. Finally Mom said, "Hm, why don't you bring Gina over after School so I could meet her. Would she come over after School?"

"I guess," I said. Nobody ever came over to my house after School and I was a little Worried that Gina wouldn't want to. And to tell the truth I felt kind of stupid asking Gina to come over so Mom could meet her. I mean it wasn't like Gina was a boy and taking me out or anything. But I knew Mom wouldn't let me go to Gina's Party if she didn't meet Gina so the next day I asked her if she could come over my house.

"Sure," Gina said. "But I have to ask my Mother."

So Gina called her Mother who said it was all right. The only thing that Worried me then was that Gina had all these cool T-Shirts with sayings on them, and that day in School she had one on that said TENNIS PLAYERS HAVE BALLS. I had only one T-Shirt with writing on it and mine said NOBODY'S PREFECT which wasn't Dirty just

Clever but Mom wouldn't even let me wear it to School. Naturally I was afraid if Mom saw Gina's TENNIS PLAYERS HAVE BALLS T-Shirt she wouldn't let me go to Gina's Party. I didn't want to say anything though, because Gina certainly had the right to wear whatever she wanted.

At first I thought maybe I could spill something on Gina's T-Shirt like Kathy spilled her soup on me that time and then Gina would have to change it but finally I came right out and told her Mom wouldn't like her T-Shirt. And that was the great thing about Gina. She knew right away what I meant because she said she really wasn't allowed to wear that T-Shirt to School because her Mother didn't like it so when she left her house that morning she covered it up with another T-Shirt.

"I'll just put on my other T-Shirt," Gina said. "It's in my Locker." If that was Allie she would of said, "Shit, Deedie, your Mother is a real Pain In The Ass if you ask me!" which might of been true but not up to Allie to point out, if you know what I mean. Anyway Gina came over to my house that afternoon and Mom gave her another Third Degree.

"Are there going to be boys at your Party?" Mom said.

"Sure," Gina said. "It's a Boy-Girl Party."

"*Nice* boys?" Mom said.

"Sure," Gina said.

"Will your Parents be home?" Mom said.

"Only my Mother," Gina said. "My Father's dead."

"Oh," Mom said.

I said "Oh" too because I didn't know Gina's Father was dead. I found out later he wasn't, but Gina's Mother and Father were Divorced and Gina didn't like him anyway. But I guess when Gina said her Father was dead Mom felt kind of bad she'd asked all those questions so she said I could go to the Party if I didn't come home too late and what time should I get picked up?

"My Mother said she'd drive anyone home who lived too far to walk," Gina said.

"That's nice," Mom said.

On Friday night I put on my NOBODY'S PREFECT T-Shirt and my old jeans but Mom said that was no way to dress for a Party.

"Nobody wears jeans to a Party," Mom said.

"Everybody wears jeans to a Party," I said.

"Then wear your new jeans," Mom said. "Didn't you get new jeans for your Birthday? Wear your new jeans."

"They're *brand*-new," I said. "They're not faded yet."

"That's why you should wear them," Mom said.

"Everybody wears *faded* jeans," I said.

"I don't care what everybody wears," Mom said. "I care what you wear. Wear your new jeans."

"Okay," I said, which may surprise you. That I gave in I mean. But I'd just remembered how come Gina could wear her TENNIS PLAYERS HAVE BALLS T-Shirt to School. She carried around another T-Shirt as a spare and changed when the Occasion demanded. So I did the same thing. I put on my new jeans that I got for my Birthday and put my faded jeans in a paper bag. When Mom was upstairs I put the paper bag outside in the bushes. Mom was letting me walk to Gina's because it was still light out. I yelled Good-bye, snuck the bag out of the bushes, and left. As soon as I got to Gina's I ran into her Bathroom and changed before anyone could see I wasn't wearing faded jeans. It was so simple. I wondered why I'd never thought of anything that simple before.

18

But when I came out of Gina's Bathroom and Gina wasn't there I got a little nervous which I hadn't had time to be up till then. I mean it was great to be invited to a Party, and it was great thinking about going to a Party, but now that I was there, all of a sudden I wished I wasn't. I just didn't know what to *do* at a Party.

So I stood outside the Bathroom door, holding the paper bag with the new jeans I got for my Birthday, when Gina's Mother came out of the Kitchen.

"Hi," said Gina's Mother. "I'm Mrs. Sarlo."

"Hi," I said. "I'm Deedie Wooster."

It must of looked like I didn't know what to do with my paper bag because Mrs. Sarlo took it right out of my hand.

"Oh, fine," Mrs. Sarlo said. "I'll take this. Thank you very much, Deedie. Why don't you go downstairs? Everybody's in the Den."

Well how could I go downstairs when Mrs. Sarlo took my paper bag? I mean I didn't care that she took it but I didn't know why she said "Thank you very much, Deedie" on top of it. So I started to Worry that maybe she thought my new jeans that I got for my Birthday were a Present for Gina. That really scared me because supposing it was *Gina's* Birthday and Gina forgot to tell me it was a Birthday Party and *God,* what would Mom say when I didn't come home with the new jeans she gave me for *my* Birthday?

I went toward the Den stairs where all the noise was coming from and I decided that I would watch for Gina's Mother and if she came downstairs to the Den I would run back up to the Kitchen where she put my paper bag and stick it outside in the bushes so I could get it when I left the Party. I'll tell you I was beginning to think that no Party in the world was worth all the Aggravation.

But just as I opened the door to the Den Mrs. Sarlo came back out of the Kitchen. She was holding my paper bag.

"There's a brand-new pair of jeans in this bag, Deedie," Mrs. Sarlo said, which I knew already.

"They're mine," I said in case she still thought they were a Birthday Present for Gina.

"Oh, I'm sorry," Mrs. Sarlo said. "I thought they were potato chips or something. Some of the kids are bringing potato chips or something."

"They are?" I said.

"Yes," Mrs. Sarlo said. "Or soda. Don't worry if you forgot. We've got enough to feed an Army."

Believe me I felt terrible. Naturally I was glad it wasn't Gina's Birthday and that I didn't forget to bring a Present but I wished I'd of known to bring potato chips or soda or something. Gina should of told me it was a Chip-In Party.

"Deedie?" Mrs. Sarlo said.

"Yes?" I said.

"What are the new jeans for?" Mrs. Sarlo said.

"Oh," I said. "In case I spill something. I brought a change in case I spill something."

I mean if I told Mrs. Sarlo I brought the new jeans I got for my Birthday because Mom wouldn't let me wear my faded jeans, the next thing I knew Mrs. Sarlo might wonder if maybe Gina did the same thing with her TENNIS PLAYERS HAVE BALLS T-Shirt and Gina would get mad at me.

"Oh," Mrs. Sarlo said and I think she looked at me kind of funny. "I'll put these with your jacket. Everybody's downstairs, Dear. Have a good time."

"Thank you," I said and figured I would sneak

out of the Party and go home when nobody was looking.

I started down the steps and would you believe that the first person I recognized was Joey Falcaro, the boy who called me Piano Legs in Gym? He was also in my English Class but fortunately my legs were covered up in English so he only called me Piano Legs when they were visible to his naked eye. Anyway I stopped dead in my tracks and almost had a Heart Attack. More than anything I wished I hadn't come to that Party. I just stood there on those steps staring down at Joey Falcaro and Joey Falcaro stared back up at me with this stupid smile on his face at all times.

Then a funny thing happened.

I have to apologize for something I'm going to do now, which is stopping my book smack in the middle of Gina's Party to tell you about my English Class. Because what happened to me and Joey Falcaro at the Party fits in perfectly with that English Class and you'll see why in a minute. All you have to do is keep that picture in your head of me at the top of the stairs to Gina's Den and Joey Falcaro at the bottom looking up. And if that makes you think of a certain Balcony Scene (very Famous!) then you won't be too far wrong.

I've mentioned that I haven't told you about my

English Class yet because so far almost everything I said about School and Teachers and my Life in General was kind of Negative and I wanted to get all those Negative things out of the way first. But my English Class was very Positive. I'll go into it more later but I have to tell you a little bit about it now so you'll understand why I had to stop here.

English was Special to me because of one person, Mr. Zachary. He was an absolutely fantastic Teacher and I don't mean just because he hardly taught Grammar and Parts Of Speech and stuff like that which is necessary to a person's Education but boring, so to speak. In fact that was one of Mom's complaints about him. She said that Mr. Zachary didn't Get Down To The Basics which she considered very important (you remember how she corrected my first book) and I'll have to be honest and say Mr. Zachary didn't do much of that.

But I judge a Teacher differently than Mom. First of all that Teacher has to like kids which Mr. Zachary did. You could see that, just by the way he talked to us. He had the same kind of feelings for kids that Mr. Oliver and Miss Offencrantz who is now Mrs. Reif did and you remember what I thought of them.

And the second way I judge a Teacher is by how much he likes what he's teaching. Now in Mr. Zachary's case he didn't only like what he taught, he *loved* what he taught. Especially when it came to a certain Author named William Shakespeare who lived (and died) quite a few years ago. Let me tell you that when Mr. Zachary talked about Mr. Shakespeare his eyes shone and his voice rang and his whole face lit up like he had a bulb in his mouth and you just *felt* how much he loved Mr. Shakespeare's Plays.

Which is why I really loved *Romeo and Juliet*. Because the way Mr. Zachary got into that Play, I just couldn't help getting into it too. And I wasn't the only one in my Class who felt that way, so did a lot of the others. There were just a couple of kids, like Joey Falcaro for one, who said Shakespeare was boring and didn't talk English (which was pretty dumb if you ask me because Shakespeare came from England) and some of the boys wrote Dirty Remarks under the pictures when Mr. Zachary wasn't looking. One boy went so far as to say Shakespeare Sucked but that boy said everything did so don't go by him.

But the way Mr. Zachary taught *Romeo and Juliet* made me a regular fan and I must of read it over a hundred times since we finished it in Class. I just wish you could of seen how Mr. Zachary jumped up on his desk when he read the Fight Scene like he really had a Sword in his hand and everything. Once he even fell off his desk and banged his head on the floor but instead of being embarrassed all he said was:

O, I am slain!

which if you know that Play is a common occurrence throughout.

To tell the truth when Mr. Zachary fell and said, " 'O, I am slain!' " we thought he really killed himself and we ran to the front of the room to pick him up but he only winked at us and burst out laughing. You can see what I mean about what a great Teacher he was. He knew Shakespeare so well that when he fell off his desk he could Quote a Line that almost fit the Situation.

So I became a Quoter myself and I memorized so many Lines that I practically knew the Play by heart and after a while I saw a million Situations where Lines from *Romeo and Juliet* came to me without even trying.

Which is what they did when I saw Joey Falcaro at Gina's Party and why I had to explain about the Party and Mr. Zachary and *Romeo and Juliet* and Joey Falcaro and my becoming a Quoter all at the same time. I would of Quoted long before this but I just didn't want you to think I was Showing Off.

I'll take you back to the Party now.

19

In case you forgot where I left off, I was standing on the top of Gina's Den stairs and Joey Falcaro was standing at the bottom and that's why I said you might of thought of a Famous Balcony Scene. Now you know I meant *Romeo and Juliet*. Except what I was actually thinking when I first saw Joey Falcaro comes a little earlier in the Play.

I don't know if you remember the part where Romeo crashes Juliet's Party. Well he was able to do that because in those days everybody wore Masks when they went to Parties, not just on Halloween, otherwise Romeo wouldn't of been able to get in. The big thing in the Play is that Romeo is a Montague and Juliet is a Capulet and the two Families have this terrible Feud going and naturally they aren't talking to each other.

And the reason Romeo Montague crashes Juliet Capulet's Party in the first place is because he expects to see another girl there named Rosaline who he happens to be in love with at the time. But while Romeo is hanging around looking for Rosaline, all of a sudden he catches sight of Juliet. Naturally Juliet doesn't know Romeo from a hole in the wall. I mean even if he wasn't wearing a Mask she wouldn't of known who he was because they'd never met, the Families having this Feud and all. And Juliet's Parents kept her very protected anyway because she was even younger than me by a couple of months. Even if there was a Hero-Burger in those days Juliet wouldn't of been allowed to hang out there, it wouldn't of mattered if it was the sides, front, or back.

Her father lets you know how old she is almost in the beginning of the Play:

> My child is yet a stranger in the world;
> She hath not seen the change of fourteen years.

(Don't let that word *hath* scare you. After a while you don't even notice words like that.)

Well as I said, Romeo suddenly sees Juliet and in two shakes of a lamb's tail he forgets that Rosaline is even alive:

Did my heart love till now? Forswear it, sight!
For I ne'er saw true beauty till this night.

Putting that in Plain English, you could see that Juliet Capulet is now the Number One girl in Romeo's life. But as luck would have it, Juliet's cousin Tybalt recognizes Romeo's voice and gets mad that Romeo crashed their Family Party and so the Feud starts up again and I won't spoil it by telling you what happens but the thing is this. There's Romeo staring at Juliet so of course Juliet stares back at Romeo and you know right away there's going to be a Tragedy. (I didn't really give away the Ending because all of Shakespeare's Tragedies end in a Tragedy.)

And the reason I thought of Romeo and Juliet when me and Joey Falcaro were staring at each other was because it was just the opposite from the Play. I mean, where Romeo and Juliet looked at each other like a TV Commercial for Italian Wine, me and Joey Falcaro looked like we were going to Throw Up. If Shakespeare would of seen us he would of said, "Well, now perchance I see'st the Plot for another Tragedie. Boy, get me my Quill!"

I looked around for Gina and even though she was sitting on the couch with a boy, I went over and sat down too. I figured I would stay just a little while longer and as soon as I could, I'd sneak upstairs, get my paper bag with the new jeans I got for my Birthday, and walk home. I'd tell Mom the Party broke up early. Except the way things turned out I didn't have to do that after all.

For one thing I didn't have to talk much because the Stereo was so loud you couldn't hear what anybody said anyway and for another thing I finally had something to do because what happened was, I had to go to the Bathroom which I always do when I'm nervous and when I came out Mrs. Sarlo gave me a bowl of potato-chip dip to pass around. That made things a little easier because when you're passing things around you don't have to stay in any one place long enough to make Conversation. Naturally I passed that potato-chip dip around to everybody except Joey Falcaro who didn't seem to notice because he was sitting in this chair with a girl on his lap and they were Making Out like crazy. Personally I couldn't see how any girl could Make Out with Joey Falcaro because not only was he Obnoxious but as I said he was very short which I guess is why he had to Make Out from a sitting position.

Anyway after I passed the potato-chip dip around which nobody wanted because by that time they were all Making Out, I passed around a dish of Chocolate-Covered Raisins which nobody wanted either. I'll tell you if you're ever at a Party and you don't know what to do with yourself because everybody's Making Out except you, you can always act Casual by passing the food around. That way people get the impression you're helping out the Hostess and you don't have time to Make Out even though you'd like to very much.

But all of a sudden somebody turned out the lights and asked who had any Grass. Well Gina didn't mind that the lights went out but she said we couldn't smoke Grass because her Mother was upstairs and anyway it was time for Kissing Games. When I heard that, I almost had another Heart Attack. Believe me there was nobody in that room I wanted to kiss and between you and me I didn't think there was anybody who wanted to kiss me. Besides I couldn't see why they had to play Kissing Games when everybody was already kissing somebody anyway.

But as soon as Gina said it was time to play Kissing Games all the kids stopped kissing so that they could suggest which Kissing Game to play.

"Run, Catch, and Make Out!"

"Spin The Bottle!"

"Seven Minutes In Heaven!"

"Seven Minutes In Heaven With *Overtime*!"

"Mix-Up!"

"Yeah! Mix-Up!"

"Yeah, yeah! *Mix-Up Mix-Up Mix-Up!*"

It was plain to see that Mix-Up was everybody's preference. Naturally I didn't make any suggestions because I didn't know Mix-Up from Seven Minutes In Heaven although I had a general idea about Spin The Bottle. What's more I was absolutely Terrified because I'd never even kissed a boy in my entire Life except for a boy cousin who has since moved to California for which I'm very grateful on account of his Roving Hands.

Somebody passed out toothpicks that were broken in half. Don't ask me how it worked because I'm not sure myself but all I'll say is before I knew what happened I was in this room off Gina's Den and I'm not kidding because you may think I'm making this up, but I was in that room with Joey Falcaro of all people. Frankly I don't think he even looked at his half of the toothpick or my half of the toothpick which wasn't exactly fair and of course I wouldn't say anything being a Guest and all but he just grabbed my hand and all of a sudden I was alone with Joey Falcaro.

When the door clicked shut the light in that room went out and I could still hear him breathing but I couldn't see him anymore. If you want to know I thought maybe he meant to grab this other girl's hand, the one he was kissing in the chair. She was a little bit shorter than me and closer to his size, and I was afraid when he found out he got me instead of her he'd say "Ech!" or something.

Believe me if he would of said "Ech!" I would of come right back with:

> Now, by the stock and honor of my kin,
> To strike him dead I hold it not a sin.

But he didn't say "Ech!" Instead he whispered, "Deedie?" and I whispered back, "Uh-huh," so that was straightened out.

And he went on breathing very hard.

20

Let me tell you how he was breathing. You know when somebody calls you on the telephone and doesn't say who it is and you can just hear them breathing? Well that's how Joey Falcaro was breathing! Kind of loud gasps and everything and to tell you the truth it sounded to me like *he* had Emphysema and I wondered if I could hold my breath if he decided to really kiss me which I doubted if he would.

So there was Joey Falcaro breathing like nobody's business and I tried to back away from his mouth because God only knew what kind of Diseases were stored up in there and that's when I realized I couldn't move back even if my Life depended on it because my head was flat against the door by then and Joey Falcaro had his hands on my shoulders like he was nailing me to that door. And on top of that he was *leaning* against me!

I mean really leaning!

Now by that time I was able to see a little better because my eyes got used to the dark and I noticed that I didn't have to hold my breath anymore even if I wanted to because Joey Falcaro's mouth only came to a little below my chin since he was so much shorter than me.

But that wasn't the only reason I didn't hold my breath anymore. This might sound kind of dumb to you because I just told you that I was Worried about Diseases but all of a sudden I not only stopped Worrying about Diseases and that included Tuberculosis along with Emphysema, but I didn't even care that Joey Falcaro called me Piano Legs in Gym.

Because right then and there with Joey Falcaro leaning against me and everything, two whole sections from *Romeo and Juliet* popped into my head at the same time and did they ever fit the Situation! I mean the Situation couldn't of been fitter if William Shakespeare had of known me and Joey Falcaro personally.

The first bunch of Lines was when Juliet discovers that Romeo is a Montague and she won't be able to go out with him because their Families are Sworn Enemies.

> My only love, sprung from my only hate!
> Too early seen unknown, and known too late!
> Prodigious birth of love it is to me
> That I must love a loathèd enemy.

Well you can see what I'm saying. There I was almost Making Out with a boy who called me Piano Legs only a couple of days before and who at the time I considered a loathèd enemy. Except that with him leaning against me the way he was I didn't think he was so loathèd anymore. (That funny little line over the *e* only means you have to give that word two Syllables instead of one, otherwise you can forget about it.)

Anyway I don't have to tell you that I was in the same State of Confusion that Juliet must of been in because how was Romeo ever going to love her if she was a Capulet, just like how could Joey Falcaro want to Make Out with a girl who had Piano Legs and was a whole head taller than him?

But before I could figure that out, the second bunch of Lines came to me right on top of the first ones. Which is when Juliet realizes that Romeo heard her calling to him from her Famous Balcony except she didn't know he was there, so naturally she was very embarrassed when he jumped out of the bushes and exposed himself. (Showed his face I mean.) So she says:

Thou know'st the mask of night is on my face,
Else would a maiden blush bepaint my cheek
For that which thou hast heard me speak tonight.

Translating that into Plain English again all Juliet meant was that if it wasn't so dark, Romeo would of been able to see how she was blushing. Which was why those Lines came to me too. Because to tell the truth my cheeks got so hot that I knew they must of been as red as a beet and if the light was on in that room Joey Falcaro would of seen just how red they were! And while I was thinking how glad I was the light was off, Joey Falcaro whispered something again in this real gravelly voice like when you've got a Strep Throat, except he was breathing so hard I couldn't understand him.

"What?" I said trying to show my annoyance because I couldn't tell what he said. (My annoyance showed by the way I said *"What?"*)

"I *said*"—Joey Falcaro whispered—"how come you didn't bring me any potato-chip dip?"

"Oh!" I whispered back. "You were busy." Which he frankly was.

"What?" Joey Falcaro whispered.

"I said you were *busy*!" I said a little louder. It looked like we were getting into a long Conversation and I wondered if we were playing Seven Minutes in Heaven With Overtime instead of Mix-Up.

"Well?" Joey Falcaro said. "Do you wanna?"

"Do I wanna what?" I said but of course I knew what he meant. I just wouldn't say it unless *he* did.

"You wanna Make Out I mean?" Joey Falcaro said.

"Oh," I said very Unconcerned. "Only if *you* wanna Make Out," which in my opinion told him exactly how I felt.

And he did so I did and all the while he was kissing me and leaning up against me (very close I might add) and breathing very hard, I got this funny feeling. It was the same kind of feeling I got squeezing my pillow, if you remember.

Not only that but I could tell something was happening to Joey Falcaro too. Gina's cousin, the one who's in Eleventh Grade, told Gina and me about this thing that happens to boys when they get Sexually Excited. It's not the Wet Dream I told you about which happens when they're asleep and dreaming, but this thing happens when a boy is kissing a girl and he's wide awake and on his toes.

In fact, Gina's cousin said, it sometimes happens even if a boy is just *thinking* about a girl! And Gina's cousin said that girls sometimes get the same kind of feeling which I already knew because of that pillow business but that you could *tell* when a boy felt like that because he gets very hard down below, if you know where I mean, and sometimes you can see a bump. The bump is called An Erection.

Well Joey Falcaro got one of those Erections and I could feel it as plain as day. Not because I tried, naturally, but as I said he was leaning up against me and if you want to know at first I thought it was the keys in his pocket or something and I was going to ask him to please put his keys in his other pocket. But all of a sudden I knew it wasn't Joey Falcaro's keys.

Before I knew it I was breathing very hard myself, and Joey Falcaro began to kiss me using the French Method and frankly he could of had the Bubonic Plague for all it mattered. I didn't care anymore that he was shorter than me so I had to bend my knees a little, and I didn't care that he had a couple of pointy hairs on his chin that were sticking in my face because even those pointy hairs felt nice.

But I don't want you to think I'm a Tramp or

anything, so I'll tell you right now that as soon as he tried to shove his hands under my NOBODY'S PREFECT T-Shirt, I pushed them away.

"Uh-*uh*!" I said. "Not *there*!" and I really meant it.

"Aw," said Joey Falcaro, and he gave me one last quick kiss on my chin which was as high as he could reach since by that time I was standing up straight again, and we went back into the room with the rest of the kids.

Before I went home I remembered to change back into the new jeans I got for my Birthday.

I had a very nice time considering it was my first Boy-Girl Party.

21

When Gina's Mother dropped me off after the Party Mom and Daddy were in the living room. Daddy wasn't home from Work when I left and I knew Mom wanted him to see how I looked.

I couldn't walk into the house with the paper bag with my faded jeans in it so I stuck it in the rubbish pail on the side of the house. I figured I'd bring it inside in the morning.

"Those new jeans look nice, Deedie," Mom said. "I think they're a little tight in the Crotch but they look very nice. Don't they look nice, Bert?"

(What with everything I've been telling you I think I forgot to mention that Daddy's name is Bert. Anyway that's who she was talking to.)

"Yes," Daddy said. "Very nice."

"Those are the new jeans Deedie got for her

Birthday," Mom said which Daddy knew because he paid for them.

"Boy, I'm tired," I said. "I better go to bed."

"Did you have a nice time, Deedie?" Mom said.

"Uh-huh," I said. "Boy, I'm tired. I better go to bed."

"Were the children nice?" Mom said.

"Uh-huh," I said.

"What did you do?" Mom said.

"Things," I said.

"Did you make any new friends?" Mom said.

"Uh-huh," I said. "I better go to—"

"Go on up to bed, Deedie," Daddy said. "You look tired."

"Okay," I said and started up the stairs.

"You do look tired," Mom said. "Do you think she's sick, Bert?"

Daddy turned up the TV.

As I closed my door I heard Mom say, "I hope she behaved herself."

A few minutes later Mom opened my door but I pretended I was asleep and she closed it again. I lay in bed for a long time just staring at the ceiling and thinking about everything that happened to me at the Party. The last thing I remembered was that I had to get that paper bag out of the rubbish pail in the morning.

* * *

But I didn't get up till late the next day which was Saturday. When I came down for Breakfast Mom gave me a little kiss that I didn't understand and she had this big smile on her face.

"You're Growing Up, Deedie," Mom said.

"I am?" I said.

"Mm-hm," Mom said. "I see you finally threw out those old jeans. The rubbish man took them already."

"He did?" I said.

"That's a sign of Maturity, Deedie," Mom said.

"It is?" I said.

After Breakfast I put my new jeans that I got for my Birthday in the washing machine. I added a whole cup of Clorox.

But I Observed a lot at that Party. Actually I Participated more than I Observed so I learned a lot too.

First of all even though I'd lost my faded jeans to the rubbish man, I'd found a way to keep Mom from going Berserk if I didn't do what she said. All I had to do was say Okay and do what I wanted anyway. Naturally I wouldn't do anything Ultra-Criminal, just stuff like wearing faded jeans when I wanted to, things like that.

I think maybe I began to wonder right then about declaring War on the Geraniums too. But I put that out of my mind. Juliet would of said:

It is too rash, too unadvised, too sudden . . . and I would of agreed with her. But I did start to think about it.

I also learned that Gina's cousin knew what she was talking about when she said that Soul-Kissing could get you Pregnant. Because when you get that funny feeling from Soul-Kissing I personally think you could get carried away and do the same things as the girls who went behind Hero-Burger. I don't know, I'm just saying, but I think that could happen very easily. And since I wasn't that kind of girl I knew I would never let any boy, even Joey Falcaro, put his hands under my NOBODY'S PREFECT T-Shirt or any other T-Shirt I happened to be wearing. So I learned that too.

But that whole Weekend I couldn't think about anything else except me and Joey Falcaro in that back room in Gina's Den. I just stayed in my room and played my Albums and every single song I played had to do with me and Joey Falcaro. I know Mom really did think I was sick because I hardly talked to her and when she asked me anything most of the time I didn't even hear her.

Until Sunday when she said, "Where *are* you, Deedie? Are you sick? Should we make an Appointment with the Doctor?"

So I perked up a little because I certainly didn't want her making any Appointments with the

Doctor. For all I knew maybe Doctors gave special kinds of tests or something and could tell if a Patient was Soul-Kissing over the Weekend.

"Maybe you picked up a Cold at that Party, Deedie," Mom said. "Was anybody sneezing at the Party?"

"No," I said. "I'm thinking about School. I have a Test tomorrow."

"Then why don't you Study?" Mom said.

"Okay," I said, which showed I was putting into Practice what I learned. So I went back up to my room and turned on my Stereo real low so Mom would think I was Studying.

On Monday morning I got up extra early and washed my hair and Blow-Dried it and dressed especially carefully and wore my NOBODY'S PREFECT T-Shirt to remind Joey Falcaro about Friday night. I covered it up first with a different shirt like Gina did so Mom couldn't see it.

I walked to School real slow so my Cowlick would stay down and while I was walking I thought about what Joey Falcaro would say as soon as he saw me.

It is my lady, O, it is my love!

Not that he'd actually use those Words exactly because he wasn't particularly crazy about Shakespeare but I knew I'd be able to tell by his face how he felt. Because the most important thing I learned at that Party was that at least Joey Falcaro knew where Deedie Wooster was.

And I knew he would never call me Piano Legs again.

Therefore I was quite surprised when he called me Piano Legs on Monday.

Well let me tell you it was a shock. But I wasn't a Quoter for nothing.

So I said, " 'What's in a name? That which we call a rose/ By any other name would smell as sweet.' "

And he said, *"Huh?"*

So I said, " 'Eyes, look your last! Arms, take your last embrace!' "

And he said, "Put a lid on it, Piano Legs!"

So I said, " 'Yea, noise? Then I'll be brief. O happy dagger! This is thy sheath.' "

And I stuck him with my pencil.

Part Two
Found

Come out, come out, wherever you are. . . .

22

Maybe if Joey Falcaro'd been a little crazier about Shakespeare he would of been able to come up with more than just "Huh?" and "Put a lid on it, Piano Legs!" but he wasn't, so he didn't, and that was the end of my first Close Brush with Sex.

Don't think I dropped dead over it. Frankly, the way he went after my NOBODY'S PREFECT T-Shirt it would of been stretched out of shape in no time and besides, it's not very Romantic having to bend your knees every time you want to kiss a person. Anyway it wasn't such a Devastating Experience considering that all I lost was my pants (the faded jeans) and now I can finally get down to telling you about Mr. Zachary and my English Class.

But I want to say something first.

I think you're going to be surprised to find a change in me. I was a little surprised myself which is why I'm telling you about it. I mean I didn't suddenly wake up one morning and say, "Well, well, Deedie Wooster, so *there* you are!" or anything like that, it was more of a gradual change sort of. It's just that by Ninth Grade I seemed to be a lot less Frantic about everything and when things happened that ordinarily would of thrown me for a loop they didn't throw me for such a loop anymore.

Like that business with Joey Falcaro for instance. Oh, sure I'll admit it was a little uncomfortable for a couple of days having to be in the same room with him but it only took an occasional Dirty Look from me to let him know he didn't have Deedie Wooster to kick around anymore. I've seen girls whose boyfriends broke up with them and you would of thought every girl in the School got a Pass to accompany her to the Bathroom where they all cried and smoked like nobody's business and it was usually a good three Periods before they were all well enough to go back to class.

Which wasn't the case with me. But every time I mentioned Mr. Zachary I kind of gave you the impression that the big change in me took place because of him. Now I'm not so sure. I don't want to take anything away from Mr. Zachary because as I said he was a Fantastic Teacher in my opinion but I'm beginning to wonder if he just didn't happen to come along at a time when I was ready for him, if you know what I mean. Maybe what happened to me would of happened anyway, I don't know, and I'm not saying it wasn't Mr. Zachary but now I'm not saying it was, either. It could of been anybody. Or anything.

Okay, now some of the things I'm going to tell you we did in his Class may sound kind of dumb to you which they did to me at first and which they did to plenty of other people including Teachers. Some of the Teachers said all we did was play in Mr. Zachary's Class but they were just jealous of him if you ask me because all the kids pleaded with their Guidance Counselor to put them in there. And I've already told you that Mom didn't like him because he didn't Get Down To The Basics.

But I loved him from the first day I walked into his room. He was very tall, with lots of gray hair and no Dandruff and he had these light blue eyes that made him look like he was laughing all the time. I mean they were a very happy blue. He had some lines in his face like most people do who work with kids all day and the lines and the gray hair fooled me at first, but when I got a closer look at him I saw he was really pretty young. The lines weren't there because of Age, they were just there, and I would of liked him even if he was as old as Daddy.

He told us he had a wonderful little Family, a three-year-old girl named Tara, a baby boy named Michael, and a wife named Alice. Which you might say was none of our business but he thought we'd be interested and he was very proud of them and he wanted us to know that.

He never got dressed up. He wore jeans (faded) every day, even on the first day of School. And he never took Attendance after that first day either but somehow he knew who was there and who wasn't and he knew all our names and never called you by somebody else's name like some Teachers do even on the *last* day of School. Personally he didn't have to take Attendance. He just trusted us not to Cut so naturally no one did. If anybody was Absent we knew they were either sick or dead, because Cutting Mr. Zachary's Class would be like staying away from your own Birthday Party.

We started the year with *Romeo and Juliet* which I told you about already and it was around the middle of October we got into what Mr. Zachary considered was the most important part of his job as an English Teacher, teaching us to Communicate with each other. He said that was the trouble with the world today, people not knowing how to Communicate, and if we learned nothing else for the whole year but learning to Communicate he would be satisfied.

Then he stood up in front of his desk and looked around the room.

"Goo!" he said which I don't have to tell you surprised everybody.

"Ga blah de boo-boo," he said which surprised us even more.

"Anyone know what I mean?" Mr. Zachary said.

No one did.

"Hm," Mr. Zachary said. "Okay, I'll try again. Ma-ma. Da-da."

"Mother? Daddy?" we said.

Mr. Zachary grinned and told us we were Brilliant.

"You see," he said, "I had to learn to say the Words you could understand, the way you did when you were babies just learning to talk. *That's* how we discovered Communication."

Well everybody turned to everyone else and said "Goo-goo" and "Blah-blah" till a boy in the back said, "Ma-ma, *Doo-doo*!" and Mr. Zachary said, "Hey, somebody better take that little feller to the Bathroom!" and everybody laughed.

All of a sudden Mr. Zachary made this terrible face at the girl next to me and we all got quiet. I looked to see what she was doing that made him so mad because I thought maybe she was writing a Note or something but she wasn't doing anything except looking back at Mr. Zachary with this scared look on her face.

"Did I frighten you, Holly?" Mr. Zachary said.

"Yes," Holly said in this real little voice.

"Why?" Mr. Zachary said.

"I don't know," Holly said.

"Did I say anything to frighten you?" Mr. Zachary said.

"No," Holly said. "You—you just—looked—"

"Angry?" Mr. Zachary said.

"Yes," Holly said.

"What made you think I was angry?" Mr. Zachary said.

"You *looked* angry!" Holly said which was how she looked now too.

"Right," Mr. Zachary said. "I *looked* angry. Very angry in fact. Without saying a Word, with just one ugly facial expression, I Communicated anger to Holly. Sorry about that, Holly, I didn't mean it one bit. But *what's* another way besides Words to Communicate? Let's hear it, Class!"

So everyone yelled, "Your face! A frown! A smile!"

"Good," Mr. Zachary said. "Now let's see how smart you *really* are. I'm going to make a lot of different faces and I want you to tell me what I'm feeling. *Communicating!* Here goes!"

And every time he made a face we yelled out what he Communicated.

Happy! Sad! Scared! Stoned!

He took off his shoes and tiptoed across the room. We said he was sneaking in his house after Mid-night.

He stumbled back across the room, bumped into his desk, knocked over his chair, and cracked his head on the Blackboard. We said he was Drunk.

He got down on one knee in front of Holly, clasped his hands together, and put this real dopey look on his face.

"You're in love!" we yelled.

"With *you*!" Mr. Zachary yelled back to the whole Class and the bell rang and believe me no-body wanted to leave.

Writing was another form of Communication, he said, and the next day we got our first big Writ-ing Assignment. Not the usual stuff like HOW I SPENT MY SUMMER VACATION, or HOW I *PLAN* TO SPEND MY S.V., and the same went for Winter or Easter or Christmas too. Which Teachers never marked, they only papered their walls with. But Mr. Zachary said he wanted to get to know us better and somehow we knew he meant it. We could of made it an Autobiography or what we wanted to be when we Grew Up or even just a particular episode that stood out in our memories.

I got a little Worried then because as I said my other Teachers mostly gave me Dittos. So I went up to Mr. Zachary and asked if I should do a Ditto or should I write a Composition too.

"Why shouldn't you write a Composition?" Mr. Zachary said.

So I said real low, "I always do Dittos."

He looked at me for a minute and then he said real low too, "Of course I expect a Composition from you, Deedie Wooster! If you can't write a Composition you shouldn't be in my Class!"

Well naturally I was glad not to be doing a Ditto in English too, so I went back to my seat and thought about what to write. I finally decided to tell about that time I was Queen Isabella and how that made me not want to be a Famous Actress anymore. I started my Scrap Copy in Class and when I got home I finished it and looked it over. I didn't like it and I knew what was wrong with it. I hadn't written it the way I wanted to.

Remember how I stopped using my Thesaurus because my Elementary Teachers didn't think I wrote my own Compositions? Well that's what I'd had in mind when I wrote that Scrap Copy. I didn't want Mr. Zachary thinking I had a Ghost Writer or something, so I'd been kind of careless and just scribbled down stuff without thinking too much.

But all of a sudden I wanted Mr. Zachary to

know I could do better. Maybe it was because he said, *If you can't write a Composition you shouldn't be in my Class!* I don't know. Or maybe it was my own Pride that bothered me, I don't know that either. Anyway I took my Thesaurus off my shelf where I'd stuck it behind some other books, and kept it on my desk while I wrote my Good Copy. I decided to use it if I really needed a good Word. Not a big Word, just a *good* Word. I got a little brave too and threw in a line about my Compulsion and how I might not Grow Up no matter how Healthy I appeared but it was nothing heavy, you understand, just the usual Adolescent Anxiety.

And I was careful to spell a couple of Words wrong here and there. Like *alot* for instance which I know are two separate Words but for some reason *a lot* of kids don't write them that way. I don't know why they don't but they don't.

On the other hand I think I do. Maybe it's like Mom with me and my commas and my *should, could,* and *would ofs.*

It's a little way to hold on to your Independence.

23

I forgot about my Composition over the Weekend because Gina's Party was that Friday night. I mean what with that Brief Encounter with Joey Falcaro in Gina's back room, and learning the Ins-and-Outs of Soul-Kissing, you might say I had more important things to think about. Naturally I was wrong, because I didn't know he'd be calling me Piano Legs again on Monday. But when Mr. Zachary came in with our Compositions, I put things in their Proper Perspective. After all, School Work was more important than a boy who was just Out For One Thing (and only came up to my knees anyway), so I concentrated all my attention on the Papers on Mr. Zachary's desk.

I wondered what mark I got.

One by one Mr. Zachary went over our Compositions and it was almost the end of the Period when he finally called me up to his desk.

"What've you got after this Class, Deedie?" he said.

"Lunch," I said.

"Would you mind waiting a minute?" Mr. Zachary said. "I'd like to discuss your Composition with you."

"Okay," I said as Calm as could be which I guess you know I wasn't.

I mean I tried like anything to remember if I wrote that Composition too well and Mr. Zachary would think I didn't write it myself or if it was so bad he'd figure that next time he'd better give me a Ditto after all. Then I thought maybe he even looked up my Records to see what was wrong with me and by the time everybody was out of the room I was afraid I was going to cry.

As soon as the door closed I said, "I wrote that Composition myself, Mr. Zachary!"

He grinned and I felt a little better. "I know that, Deedie," he said. "There are just a couple of Inconsistencies here I want to ask you about."

"Inconsistencies?" I said.

"Yup," Mr. Zachary said and he started looking through my Composition.

"What kind of Inconsistencies?" I said.

"Well now let's see," Mr. Zachary said. "Here's one. How do you spell 'embarrassed,' Deedie?"

I couldn't remember if that was one of the words I'd spelled right or wrong.

"I'm not sure," I said. "E-m-b-a-r-r-a-s-s-e-d?"

"Ah," Mr. Zachary said. "That's what I thought. Why did you spell it wrong in your Composition?"

"I didn't know how," I said.

"But you spelled it correctly elsewhere, Deedie," Mr. Zachary said. "In the same Composition."

"Mm," I said. "I figured I'd spell it both ways just in case, Mr. Zachary."

"I see," Mr. Zachary said.

"That way it would only be wrong once instead of twice," I said.

"I see," Mr. Zachary said.

"Mm," I said.

"Mm," Mr. Zachary said. "How about 'impression'?"

"Same reason," I said.

"Uh-huh," Mr. Zachary said. "And 'a lot'?"

I shrugged my shoulders like I did with Guidance Counselors. "I guess," I said.

Mr. Zachary said, "Deedie, you didn't spell those words wrong on purpose, did you?"

"Why would I do that, Mr. Zachary?" I said.

"I don't know," Mr. Zachary said. "That's what I'm trying to understand. Because you have a Flair for Words, Deedie, I can see that."

"I guess," I said.

"So-o-o . . ." Mr. Zachary said, "it would be kind of stupid for you to spell those words wrong when you really know how to spell them, don't you think so?"

"I guess," I said.

"Do you use a Dictionary when you write?" Mr. Zachary said.

"Uh-huh," I said.

"How about a Thesaurus?" Mr. Zachary said.

"Uh-huh—a *what*?" I said.

"A Thesaurus," Mr. Zachary said. "Every would-be Writer's got to have a copy of a Thesaurus."

"Uh-huh," I said.

"Oh, one more thing, Deedie," Mr. Zachary said. "In one part of your Composition you mentioned something about . . . Mm . . . 'when and if I Grow Up' I think you said. Something about Health?"

"Uh-huh," I said.

"Are you Worried about anything in particular?" Mr. Zachary said.

"No," I said.

"Then why did you mention it?" Mr. Zachary said.

"To fill up the pages," I said.

"I see," Mr. Zachary said. "Well I'd like you to remember something, Deedie. Being able to Write well is a fine talent. But don't cop out by hiding behind the Written Word. Don't hint, in the hope that someone will pick it up. If you've got something to say, say it. Use your Flair for Words verbally too, okay?"

"Okay," I said.

"And I want you to know I've got a good ear," Mr. Zachary said.

"A 'good ear'?" I said.

"Yup. A good ear. I can hear you. You're making some kind of noises inside you, Deedie, and I can hear you. If you should decide to talk to me sometime, just remember that I've got a good ear."

"Uh-huh," I said.

"And by the way," Mr. Zachary said. "I've got an extra Thesaurus. Suppose you borrow it till you get one of your own, all right?"

I picked my books up and walked to the door. "That's okay, Mr. Zachary," I said. "I think I have one someplace in my room."

Mr. Zachary nodded his head. "I thought you

might, Deedie. Use it from now on, will you? And remember what I said. I like the noises you're making. Just turn up your Volume a little. You're an interesting kid, Deedie Wooster."

I ran all the way to the Cafeteria.

I didn't see Gina when I got to the table we usually sat at and I knew she must of gone home for Lunch. But I saw Allie. We hadn't had Lunch together since she became President of The Sexy Seven. She was alone that day because the other six got suspended for Cutting again. Allie never got caught.

"What's doing?" Allie said.

I told her about the Composition I wrote for Mr. Zachary and that he said it was very good. Then I told her what he'd said about having a good ear and all that and that he liked the noises I was making which sounded kind of dumb when I repeated it to Allie even though it didn't sound dumb when Mr. Zachary said it.

"I think what he meant, Allie, was that if I had any Problems I could talk to him. That's what he meant when he said he had a good ear."

"He's just Nosy," Allie said. "Maybe he really wants to be a Shrink and not an English Teacher. He sounds plain Nosy if you ask me."

Which I didn't ask her so I said, "*I* think he's a very good English Teacher."

"Well I don't," Allie said. "He only wants to Gain Your Confidence and find out your True Feelings and then he'll tell your Parents so if I were you I wouldn't tell him anything."

"Mr. Zachary wouldn't do that," I said.

"Oh yeah?" Allie said. "How do you know? And he'll tell the other Teachers too. So you better watch what you say, Deedie, and I wouldn't trust him, he's pure Bullshit. The trouble with you, Deedie, is you don't recognize Bullshit when you see it."

And the trouble with Allie was that she didn't trust anybody. I told her so and she agreed. She said she felt that way ever since she found out that Thomas Jefferson had Slaves and Syphilis and that surprised me. Not that she didn't trust anybody, I knew that already. But frankly I was surprised that Thos. Jefferson would of had either Slaves *or* Syphilis and he had both.

We had an argument about that which I'd been doing a lot of lately, arguing with Allie I mean, and then I told her she shouldn't of joined The Sexy Six which was now The Sexy Seven and she said I was getting to be a Wholesale Fag and I said there were a lot of Wholesale Fags in this World and she said that at least T. Jefferson wasn't a Fag and I said he was *so* which was how he got to be President and anybody who got to be President of *anything* was a Fag and she said would I bring in those Pills my Mother kept in her night table and I said no so she said I should Shove It and I picked up my tray and said Good-bye.

"Good-bye!" Allie said. "And you better learn to recognize Bullshit when you see it, Deedie Wooster!"

That was the last Meaningful Conversation we had.

24

I got another chance to show Mr. Zachary I could do better than I did on my first Composition because for our next Assignment we had to do a Book Report. Naturally I didn't make any errors On Purpose this time and I wasn't afraid to use my Thesaurus. But we weren't allowed to write a Summary of the book, we had to tell about the one part we liked best and why that particular part had meaning for us.

I chose *Little Women* because it happened to of been my favorite book of all times and also because there was a part in it that just about killed me every time I read it. I mean I liked the whole book because the Marches were such a Loving Family and all, and I like to read about Loving Families, but they had very real Problems too, which you saw when this terrible thing happened to Beth. And even though it was the best part in the book for me it was also the worst. For Beth too, because she died.

I don't know if I told you how I cried when Ritchie died but the thing was that one day when Mom found me crying she said, "Deedie, this is How It Is. Life isn't a Book. People have a way of dying in real life. It's only in Books that everything comes out all right."

So when Beth died, naturally I felt like the Author had played this real dirty trick on me which I told Mr. Zachary in my Report and I explained that that was why Beth's dying like that had meaning for me. I mean I kept expecting her to open her eyes and say she'd been Faking all along which for a long time I used to pretend Ritchie was doing.

Because it was true. Nobody, but *nobody*, in any book I'd read up till that time, ever died. They might of got sick or something or maybe lost in the woods and Over-Exposed, and even though the Author let you *think* the person would die he never did.

I wish I had that book here now so that I could copy down the part I mean. But unfortunately it was one of the things I loaned Lisa, the girl who lived next door that I stole the Four-Color Ball-

Point pen from. She said she gave me back my *Little Women* but she didn't. When I found out she was moving, I told Mom I was going over to Lisa's house to get my book.

"After what you did over there?" Mom said. "Don't you dare!"

"But she's got my *Little Women*!" I said.

"And you stole her pen!" Mom said.

"I gave it back, didn't I?" I said.

"A nice child like Lisa!" Mom said. "You should be ashamed of yourself!"

That's when I should of told Mom that it was a "nice child like Lisa" who was Screwing Up the Inventory in Department Stores, but Mom would of thought I was trying to get even with Lisa for keeping my *Little Women*, so I didn't. I did go over there a couple of days before she moved just to say Good-bye and see if I couldn't steal my book back but everything was packed already. Besides, they watched me like Hawks.

But it doesn't matter anyway because I almost remember that part Word for Word. I'll tell you about it so maybe you'll understand why it was such a shock to me.

It seems that a lot of people were sick with Scarlet Fever in the Marches' neighborhood (I think it was Scarlet Fever but that's one of the things I'm not sure of which is why I wish I still had the book) and Mrs. March was going around delivering Hot Soup and in general taking care of everybody.

But Beth wanted to help too even though she was a Very Frail Child and while she was helping, she came down with Scarlet Fever also (if that's what it was). Well naturally I felt bad that Beth got sick but I didn't think too much of it at the time because it wasn't Real Life, and I figured any second she would make a Remarkable Recovery.

So there I was curled up on the couch, very relaxed, which you would think I had every right to be since I was only Reading for Enjoyment, when all of a sudden I came across these words (or almost these words because that Crook still has my book):

> . . . and in the dark hour before the dawn, in the room where Beth had drawn her first breath she now drew her last, with no good-bye, only a loving look and a little sigh.

I started to go on to the next paragraph when I just stopped dead. I mean I could feel my eyes open wide and I knew I made a loud Gasp because Mom said, "What's the matter?"

I couldn't answer her. I looked back at the Words and read them again.

> . . . in the room where Beth had drawn her first breath she now drew her last . . .

I turned back a page and started that part all over again. I was rubbing my hands against my legs all the time I was reading and I heard Mom ask me if I was cold but her voice sounded a million miles away from me. And then, just before I got to those last Words I covered them with my hand and only let my eyes go down the page line by line and I wouldn't pick up my fingers till I finished the line ahead of it. When there was one line to go I took my fingers away a fraction at a time and closed my eyes. I even said a little Prayer before I looked down at the page again. But there it was:

> . . . in the room where Beth had drawn her first breath she now drew her last . . .

I couldn't believe it.

"She died?" I said. "Beth *died*?"

"Didn't you know that?" Mom said.

"How could they let her die?" I yelled.

"It's only a Book, Deedie," Mom said.

"Then why did they let her die?" I yelled.

"How can you Carry On that way over a Book?" Mom said.

I cried for hours.

Mom never understood why, though, and I couldn't explain that people should die either in Real Life or in Books. One or the other.

Never in both.

I told about Ritchie in my Report and Mr. Zachary understood. I wasn't only crying for Beth.

I'm beginning to hear you better now, he wrote on that Paper. *You're making beautiful noises, Deedie Wooster!*

25

We performed an Experiment in Class one day. The Experiment had to do with Words. But I better warn you. This was one of those Freaky things we did in Mr. Zachary's Class from time to time that I said might sound dumb to you but in my case the Experiment got me to thinking about Words again and how some Words were important to me that shouldn't of been and Vice Versa.

Mr. Zachary said that people found it too easy to say things they shouldn't and when it came to saying things they should they got a mouthful of marbles all of a sudden. He told us that Words were just a combination of letters that only took on meaning when they had a Purpose which was why some Words meant one thing to one person and something entirely different to another.

"I think we should practice the Words we don't like to use until they come a little easier," Mr. Zachary said.

"I can say anything!" Joey Falcaro said and he looked at me. I looked back. I still couldn't raise my eyebrow so I held my nose which told him almost the same thing. Because he'd been annoying me again. Not that he called me names exactly but once in a while I'd take a peek at him and catch him grinning at me like the Village Idiot. It was very irritating.

"It's what a person thinks and feels that makes his Words important," Mr. Zachary said. "Suppose I give you people three Words to say to anyone in this room. Three Words, remember, that are just a combination of letters, or Symbols really, that don't mean anything unless you want them to. You'll just be following my instructions and repeating those Words. Understand?"

"What are the Words?" Gina said.

"Now hold on a minute," Mr. Zachary said. "Let's get that straight. Those three Words will have no significance whatsoever because the person speaking does not mean what those Words usually express! Have you got that?"

"We'll only be kidding, right?" Joey Falcaro said.

"Right," Mr. Zachary said. "Just a combination

of Symbols I've given you to repeat. Let me caution you though. Even though you'll only be kidding, you're still going to have a tough time getting those Words out."

"What are the Words?" Larry Berman said.

"Well one more thing before we start. *Everyone* in this room must be approached with the Words. As soon as one of you receives the Words you have to say them to someone who *hasn't* received them, no matter who's left. Okay?"

"Can I go first?" Gina said.

"Why?" Mr. Zachary said.

"So I can pick anybody I want," Gina said.

"Sure," Mr. Zachary said. "Does anyone object if Gina goes first?"

Naturally I would of liked to go first for the same reason as Gina but I didn't object out loud. Neither did anyone else.

"All right then," Mr. Zachary said. "Let's put our chairs in a Circle. Larry, slide my chair in somewhere, will you?"

A boy named Paul said, "Are you in this too?"

"Of course," Mr. Zachary said. "I wouldn't ask you to do anything I wouldn't do. Get moving, everybody."

When we finally stopped sliding our chairs around, Mr. Zachary sat down in his chair between Paul and this super-quiet girl named Trish.

"Now, Gina," Mr. Zachary said, "this is the Procedure. You're to get up, walk to the middle of the Circle until you decide whom you've chosen. Then you walk over to that person, address that person by name, and say the three Words. Okay?"

"Okay," Gina said. "What are the Words?"

"And remember," Mr. Zachary said. "They're just Symbols, combinations of letters. Everybody understand?"

"Yeah, yeah, we understand!"

"Hurry up, the Period's almost over!"

"What are the Words?" Gina said.

"Oh, for Pete's Sake!" Mr. Zachary said. "I forgot to tell you, didn't I? The three Words are 'I-love-you.' "

Well you would of thought that the entire Class dropped dead of Malaria.

"'I love you'?" Gina said. "*Those* are the Words?"

"Go!" Mr. Zachary said, and he looked at his watch.

Believe me I was glad I didn't Volunteer first after all. I mean who wants to walk up to another kid in your Class and say "I love you" just like that? But Gina got up and walked to the middle of the Circle and looked at everybody real hard like it was a Tremendous Decision which of course it was. She kept turning around and around and once she looked at me but I shook my head and stared down at my desk so she wouldn't pick me. Finally she walked over to Barbara Levy.

"Barbara?" Gina said in this real shaky voice. "I— I love you." And she sat down.

Barbara looked over at Gina like she didn't think she heard right. It got so quiet in that room you would of thought the Principal was Making his Rounds. Then Larry Berman fell off his chair and everybody broke up.

"Lezzie! Lezzie!" he yelled so Gina told him to shut up, that it didn't mean you were a Lezzie just because another girl told you "I love you" when she was only following instructions.

"That's right, Larry," Mr. Zachary said. "Gina understands what we're doing here. Okay, Barbara, your turn."

So Barbara got up and walked to the middle of the Circle and turned around and around like Gina did till all of a sudden she walked over to Larry Berman, and said, "Larry, you Creep, I love you!" And she ran back to her seat.

Mr. Zachary laughed. "Not quite," he said, "but very understandable. Go ahead, Larry."

I guess everybody figured the best thing to do was get the "I love you" over with but whoever stepped into the Circle took so long to make a choice it looked like they were considering a Permanent Arrangement. At last it went from Larry to Susan to Mr. Zachary to Holly to Paul and around the room real slow like that till it was finally said to Joey Falcaro and by that time the only ones left in the room were me and this boy named Mark Daly.

You could see Joey Falcaro's problem. He and I hadn't said even one word to each other since he said, "Put a lid on it, Piano Legs!" and I stuck him with my pencil. But if he said "I love you" to Mark Daly he was afraid Larry would of yelled "Queer!" at him and Joey Falcaro had to think of his Reputation. So he just kept turning around in the middle of the room and first he looked at Mark and then he looked at me and then he looked at Mr. Zachary and then he looked back at me again.

I felt my heart banging away like crazy and all of a sudden I thought, *Oh, God, nobody's going to say "I love you" to Faggy Deedie Wooster, not even Joey Falcaro!* and I looked up at the Clock hoping the bell would ring and Mark looked up at the Clock and Joey Falcaro looked up at the Clock and we all knew there was at least a hundred years left in the Period.

"I don't have to mean it, right?" Joey Falcaro finally said, and I'm glad to tell you his voice cracked in the middle.

"I thought that was understood," Mr. Zachary said.

"Just so we got that straight," Joey Falcaro said.

"*We've* got it straight," said Mr. Zachary. "Have you?"

"Okay," Joey Falcaro said.

"Okay," Mr. Zachary said.

"Okay!" Joey Falcaro said.

And before I knew what happened there was Joey Falcaro glaring down at me like he could kill me.

"DeedieohGodoh*Jesus*whata*Crock*thisisDeedieI-loveyou!"

Well as Cool as a Cucumber I got up and walked over to Mark Daly. "Mark?" I said. "It's a pleasure to tell you 'I love you'!"

And it was all over.

Naturally everybody had a million questions. "What'd *that* prove?" "Why are we *doing* this?" "What's this got to do with *English*?"

But Mr. Zachary only looked at his watch again and wrote the time down on a piece of paper.

"Well," he said, "I was just trying to show you how difficult it is to say three very sensitive Words even though I stated *specifically* that you didn't mean them at all. But most of you still found them almost impossible to get out. Now I'm going to change *one* of those Words and I think you'll get the significance of what we did today. I'll start this time."

He checked his watch, got up out of his chair, and

walked over to Holly. "Holly, I hate you," Mr. Zachary said, "and I'm sure you know I don't mean that."

Everybody laughed and Holly jumped right up, walked over to Gina, and said, "Gina, I hate you."

Before you looked around, everybody had "hated" everyone else.

Mr. Zachary walked into the center of the Circle.

"Now, despite the fact that I assured you we didn't mean one Word that was said, it took, let's see . . . more than twenty minutes to get through 'I love you,' and not even *one* minute for everyone to say 'I hate you.' Just Symbols, I said. Combinations of letters. No meaning. No significance. What do *you* suppose it meant, Class?"

We all stared at him.

"Think about it when you leave here today. *I* think it's a little sad, don't you?"

We were all kind of quiet as we left the room.

Because it *was* sad, if you know what I mean.

I thought about other combinations of letters.

Only eight Symbols in both of them.

G-E-R-A-N-I-U-M.

T-W-O-I-N-O-N-E.

They were sad too.

26

A few weeks before Christmas Mr. Zachary announced we were going to have a Holiday Party and to show you how Wrapped-Up I was in that Class, I'd forgotten to start Worrying about Christmas. I mean usually very early in December, or sometimes in the middle of November even, I'd begin to get this squirmy feeling in my stomach because Christmas meant Presents and Presents meant Cards and Cards meant I was Mom's little Two-In-One again.

I mean I could see me fifty years from now, with straggly white hair and wrinkles all over and I would still be a dumb Two-In-One in a wheelchair with Mom's Geranium in my lap.

So when Mr. Zachary talked about a Holiday

Party I pushed the squirmy feeling away. It was beginning to annoy me. But even a Holiday Party in Mr. Zachary's Class was a different Experience and he said we had to make Special Plans for it which we were just about to do when Mr. Baxter the Principal came in.

Naturally Mr. Baxter said he was Just Visiting but everybody knew when the Principal came into your room he was really Observing the Teacher. Because when that happened the Teacher who was being Observed got very Professional all of a sudden and wrote lots of stuff on the Board which ordinarily he never did because the kids always stole the Chalk. Or he'd get Over-Polite and say things like "Yes, Young Lady" or "Let's work as quietly as we *usually* do, *shall* we?" Sometimes a Teacher got so nervous he'd tell us to take out our Homework which made the Situation a little tricky since he didn't give any, and which we reminded him of in very strong language, Princ. or no Princ. I mean there's a limit.

But Mr. Zachary didn't act any different when Mr. Baxter came in that day. He didn't get all choked-up like the other Teachers did or go running around looking to borrow a Polyester Jacket to wear over his jeans. And it wasn't that he didn't know Mr. Baxter was coming, either, because he said, "Ah, come in, Mr. Baxter, I've been expecting you! Class, you all know our Principal, Mr. Baxter?"

Well of course we all said Yes even though it wasn't true because frankly we didn't know him well at all. Neither did the Teachers. I once heard Mrs. Ingleholtz say that the School Board could of put a stuffed Panda in the Principal's Office and it would of served the same purpose and been twice as Decorative.

Because if you want to know we never saw Mr. Baxter unless we happened to run across him when he was coming in or going out of the building or if he called a Special Assembly to get to the bottom of the Obscene Calls that were reported to be tying up the Nurse's phone again. I once saw him pushing a TV Set down the hall and to tell the truth I thought he was one of the Custodians. It turned out he was taking the TV into his Office (it was during the World Series) and don't think the Teachers didn't make a few remarks about that.

Sometimes we saw him when he strolled into Miss Lutz's room (young Math Teacher, wore Revealing Tops) because he strolled in there pretty often and there was even some talk that Mr. Baxter had a thing going with Miss Lutz. In that case I guess he really *was* Observing Miss Lutz but she Observed him plenty too, because every day she brought her lunch into his Office so they could eat together and for that whole Period you couldn't interrupt Mr. Baxter even if the School was on fire which occasionally it was.

Anyway we all said Hello to Mr. Baxter and he sat down in the back of the room. But Mr. Zachary said we still had to make Plans for our Holiday Party so we should get into a Circle and he told Mr. Baxter to get into the Circle too. It was common knowledge that whoever sat in on Mr. Zachary's Class had to Participate in the day's activity which I guess Mr. Baxter didn't count on when he came in. Sometimes the day's activity was considered kind of Strange.

So at first we thought Mr. Baxter would say he'd prefer to Visit on another day. I mean he had this startled look on his face like he swallowed a fish bone and he sort of froze in his seat in the back of the room. But Mr. Zachary didn't seem to notice that, he just said, "Now look, kids, I don't want you to be inhibited because Mr. Baxter is here today. He wants you to be relaxed in his Presence, don't you, Mr. Baxter?"

"Certainly," Mr. Baxter said. "Certainly."

But after he said Certainly four more times he still hadn't moved his chair and by that time he was the only one left out of the Circle. I felt kind of bad that he was all alone back there because he looked like a little kid that nobody would let into the Sandbox. So I moved my chair next to his and I'll tell you he smiled at me like I'd just said I'd be his Best Friend.

There was an embarrassing moment though, because Mr. Baxter and I both happened to notice there was writing on the desk he was sitting at. Somebody had scribbled *Grateful Dead* and right under that *This School Sucks,* which I guess was News to Mr. Baxter because he looked sort of Depressed. I rubbed off *This School Sucks* with a little bit of spit and told Mr. Baxter not to Worry, there was a boy in the Class who said everything did. I left on *Grateful Dead* even though they're not my favorite Group.

"Thank you," Mr. Baxter said.

"You're Welcome," I said, and we both looked back at Mr. Zachary.

The Plans for our Holiday Party went like this. Each of us had to tell the Class something we'd like very much to have, or what we wanted to be, or maybe someplace special in the World we would like to go. And as each person spoke we had to listen very carefully and if we didn't hear what they said we could say "What?" only once and that person would have to say his Hope a little louder. Then we would go on to the next person.

Somebody, Gina I think, wanted a house near

the ocean all by herself where the only people allowed were under twenty years old. Somebody else wanted a million dollars to donate to medical research. Joey Falcaro wanted a harem.

While the rest of the Class was expressing its Hopes I stole a peek at Mr. Baxter. I was afraid any minute he'd say, "Here, here, Mr. Zachary, what's this got to do with English? Why aren't you Getting Down To The Basics?" But he didn't. As a matter of fact he stopped looking scared and you could see he was having as good a time as everybody else.

Then Mr. Zachary said, "And what's *your* Pleasure, Mr. Baxter?"

So Mr. Baxter said "Oh!" like it never occurred to him that anyone was really interested in knowing what *he* wanted but since I was sitting right next to him I heard him breathe in, like somebody punched him in the stomach. Then he grinned and kind of puffed out his chest because he was pleased to be included after all and I'll tell you, it would of Fit the Situation perfectly if he said, *It is an honor I dreamed not of,* but he wasn't a Quoter I guess, being a Principal and not an English Teacher.

Finally he said, "Why, I—I suppose . . . Mm . . . flowers would be nice. Yes, flowers. To dress up my Office? Yes, I would say flowers."

When we all finished expressing our Hopes, Mr. Zachary said, "Now the point here is that I wanted you all to become aware of your Classmates' Aspirations. Each one of you has Communicated something to this Class. It's up to the rest of you to remember it. What you're going to do now is write your name and telephone number on a slip of paper, fold it up, and when I come around the room you're going to drop the paper in this box."

He took a little box out of his filing cabinet and put it on his desk. Then he explained he would call us up to his desk one by one and we had to take out one of the slips of paper. We were allowed to look at it to make sure we didn't get our own, and if we did we could pick a different one.

"And that person will be your Secret Pal," Mr. Zachary said.

"Secret Pal?"

"What's this got to do with Communicating?"

"Huh?" (Guess who.)

So Mr. Zachary said that suppose our Secret Pal wants to Travel, for example, then we should bring in Folders and stuff with pictures of where he wants to go. Or if our Secret Pal wants to be a Scientist, we had to look through Newspapers or Magazines for Articles on Science. And if we couldn't find anything Scientific, we should just use our Imaginations and bring in anything lying around the house that could apply to our Secret Pal.

"Ask first though, if it doesn't belong to you," Mr. Zachary said. "Don't bring in any Family Heirlooms, okay?"

We weren't allowed to buy wrapping-paper either, we could only use the Sunday Funnies or even a cut-up Grocery bag because Mr. Zachary said that how it was wrapped didn't mean anything. It was what was inside that showed how much thought we'd be giving to our Secret Pal.

"What do we need the phone number for?" someone said.

"Ah," Mr. Zachary said. "I was wondering when you'd get around to that. If you remember, I told you that your Mission for the week is to give your Secret Pal something to do with his Aspiration. But it's also to make that person happy!"

"I'm not allowed to give our phone number out," Holly said. "It's Unlisted."

"Okay," Mr. Zachary said, "then don't. Just put your name on the piece of paper." He looked over at Mr. Baxter. "As a matter of fact I think we'll spare Mr. Baxter the phone calls *and* the gift-giving. He's got enough to keep him busy without that. But if one of you would like to, you might bring something in for him as a token, okay?"

We all said Okay and I thought it was pretty shrewd of Mr. Zachary not to make Mr. Baxter give out his phone number. The next thing you knew the boy in my Class who said everything Sucked would call Mr. Baxter up and tell him he did too.

Gina said, "What should we say when we call up?"

"Well first of all," Mr. Zachary said, "you'll have to disguise your voice so your Secret Pal doesn't recognize it. Or ask someone at home to make the call for you. And then say something nice, like . . . oh, 'Don't forget to study for the Science Test tomorrow. I want you to Pass for a change.' Something like that."

So everybody said we should get started and Mr. Zachary warned us first that if we picked someone we didn't want, we weren't allowed to make a face or anything, it was just for the week and we were all friends in there, weren't we, so we said, Yes, let's get started.

While everyone was picking their Secret Pals out of the box I whispered to Mr. Baxter, "Does that include Geraniums?"

"What?" Mr. Baxter whispered back.

"Flowers," I said. "You told us you liked flowers for your Office. Does that include Geraniums?"

"Geraniums?" Mr. Baxter said. "Oh, *Geraniums*!

Why, yes. Yes, I suppose it does." A few minutes later he looked at me and said "Geraniums" again but he didn't have to remind me. I wasn't about to forget, if you know what I mean.

When it was my turn I hoped like anything I wouldn't get Joey Falcaro because believe me I'd drop dead before I called him up to say anything nice. But I got Paul who'd said he wanted to be a Doctor. I was glad for two reasons. First because it wasn't Joey Falcaro and second because I still had so many Pills at home I could bring him one a day for a whole year without making a dent in our Medicine Cabinet.

I wondered who got my name. I'd said I wanted to be a Writer. I hoped whoever was my Secret Pal had heard me. Frankly I'd said it kind of low.

And nobody had said "What?" either.

27

When I got home from School I asked Mom if she had a Geranium to spare.

"What for?" Mom said.

"For Mr. Baxter," I said.

"The Principal, you mean?" Mom said.

"Uh-huh," I said. "He likes Geraniums. He hinted he'd like me to bring him a couple."

"A *couple*?" Mom said.

"I told him only one," I said.

But you could see Mom was pleased. If you want to know she didn't seem to waste any time scooting into the Living Room to pick one out. I wasn't actually sure so I couldn't of sworn to it but I even think she said, "One less to water, Thank God!" while she was in there.

When she was back in the kitchen she said, "Are you Getting Down To The Basics in that Class?"

"Uh-huh," I said.

"Good," Mom said.

That night the phone rang while we were having Dinner. Mom answered it.

"Who is this please?" Mom said. *"Who?"*

She slammed the phone back on the hook.

"Who was it?" Daddy said.

"I don't know," Mom said. "A squeaky voice. It sounded like a kid."

All of a sudden it hit me. I'd forgotten about the phone calls. I'd been concentrating on the Presents.

"My Secret Pal!" I said.

"Your *who*?" Mom said.

The phone rang again.

"I'll get it!" I said and I picked it up. "Hello?"

"Deedie?" this squeaky voice said.

"Uh-huh?" I said.

"Are you having Dinner?" the voice said.

"Uh-huh," I said. I started to giggle.

The voice giggled too. "Well I want you to be a very good little girl and eat all your vegetables tonight. You want to be Healthy, don't you?"

"Uh-huh," I said and we both giggled again and hung up.

"*Who* was that?" Mom said.

"My Secret Pal," I said.

"What in the world is that?" Mom said.

So I explained how Mr. Zachary was teaching us to Communicate and how we had to make our Secret Pal happy for a week because that was our Mission and . . . but you know how it is when you try to explain something like that. It never comes out right.

"Basics, huh?" Mom said.

What did I tell you?

But Daddy liked the idea and he talked on the phone for me after I dialed Paul's number. He told Paul he should study hard if he wanted to be a Doctor and would he please not take Wednesdays off because everybody knew that Wednesday was the day people were inclined to get sick and maybe Paul could discuss that at his first Medical Convention. Mom burst out laughing at that and I must of had a surprised look on my face because she said, "What's the matter *now,* Deedie?"

"Nothing," I said. But something was. Because I'd got the same kind of feeling I did when I realized Miss Offencrantz knew I hadn't caught that bird the way I said I did.

What happened was I began to realize something about Mom too. I'd always thought Mom was too busy missing Ritchie to laugh about anything with me. And all of a sudden it hit me that maybe I'd just never noticed when Mom laughed with me. Maybe I was too busy Worrying about how Mom was too busy missing Ritchie and I never *let* myself notice an important thing like that.

It was kind of a Discovery about myself too, knowing all along that Mom might be thinking about me a lot more than I imagined she did. The Discovery didn't make me feel good either. It was very comfortable blaming everything that was wrong with me on Mom.

I stopped thinking about it.

I brought the Geranium to School the next day and took it to Mr. Baxter in his Office. He thanked me and put it very carefully on a corner of his desk. Somehow it looked different there than it did in my Living Room.

"Would you like another one?" I said.

"Oh, no," Mr. Baxter said. "One will be quite sufficient, thank you."

Which was exactly how *I* felt.

Well each day I brought in some Medical things for Paul. Besides a bottle of Vitamin Pills and left-over Calcium Tablets from my youth, I found an Article on Bill Baird's Abortion Clinic (which was in the News because someone tried to abolish it with a Bomb), an Ad for a "Discreet VD Examination: Free," an Appointment Card from Dr. Robard our Family Doctor, and a little pad from Daddy's Office for Paul to write Prescriptions on.

And I got an old Spiral Book with some empty pages that I could still write on, a soft-cover Dictionary without the soft cover, two Ball-Point pens (not Four-Color), a package of only partly rusted paper clips, and a page from a Writer's Magazine with pictures of books from the Book-of-the-Month Club. My Secret Pal had put a Circle around a book called *One Way to Write Your Novel.*

Every day was like Christmas. We snuck our Presents onto Mr. Zachary's desk when we came in, and as soon as we were in the Circle Mr. Zachary called our names and we went up to get our Presents. But we all waited as each person opened his gift to see if the Present matched that person's Aspiration.

And they did! Everyone said *"Oh!"* and *"Ah!"* and "Isn't this *great*?" and "This is the best Class in the *World*!" Because we knew it was, and you could just feel how happy we'd made each other. Even Mr. Baxter gave up his Lunch Period with Miss Lutz and brought a brand-new set of Literature Books which we all said with a straight face we needed desperately.

On the last day Mr. Zachary said it was time for us to Reveal our Identities so we could thank one another. Because up till that time we could only say "Thank you, Secret Pal" to nobody in particular. Which was the point he said. All Mr. Zachary wanted us to know was that at least one person in that room cared enough to make us happy even for only one week.

So he called our names and we had to get up, walk over to the person we'd been bringing stuff to all week, and introduce ourselves as the Secret Pal and add something nice.

When it was my turn I went to Paul and said, "I'm your Secret Pal and I know you'll be a Successful Surgeon some day." I was Worried Paul would be disappointed when he found out it was only me, but you should of seen his eyes light up.

Which was how mine did when Trish said to me, "Deedie? I'm your Secret Pal! Will you remember me when you're a Famous Writer?" And of course I knew I would even though I'd hardly noticed Trish in that room before.

Well let me tell you that everybody's eyes were shining so bright you would of thought we had a human Christmas Tree in there.

But the best part as far as I was concerned was that for the first time since Ritchie died, I liked opening Christmas Presents again.

* * *

I made myself remember that Party all the time we were home on our ten-day Vacation. Especially on Christmas Day when I opened Mom's Card.

Merry Christmas, my little Two-In-One. Love, Mom

When she wasn't looking I tore it up and threw it in the Garbage.

And this time I really did get calls from kids during Christmas Recess. Not like before when they only wanted to talk to Kristy McNichol who I guess never got my letter. (Or maybe she's In Production again which I wouldn't know because I don't watch her Program anymore.)

But Holly called me and so did Gina and Susan and I think Paul must of called a million times to thank me for all the Medical Supplies I gave him. He also said if I ever need an Operation which he hoped I wouldn't he would do it for Free because I was the one who got him started. Mom said she'd heard that before but I think it was a nice gesture.

And . . . would you *believe* that Joey Falcaro called me up also and had the nerve to say he *liked* me and wanted to go *out*?

"Yeah," said Joey Falcaro. "I—uh . . . *like* you, Deedie—"

" 'Speakest thou from thy heart?' " I said.

"Huh?" said Joey Falcaro. "Oh, yeah, yeah. Listen, Deedie, I—"

" 'By whose direction found'st thou out this place?' " I said.

"Huh?" he said. "Oh!" he said. "Well, I—uh—sort of looked through all the—uh—Woosters, and uh—you wanna go out with me hey?"

" 'And, if we meet,' " said I, " 'we shall not 'scape a brawl/ For now, these days, is the mad blood stirring.' "

"Huh?" said Joey Falcaro. "Oh, yeah, I know, I—uh, guess you're mad 'cause I called you—uh—Piano Legs, right? Uh—look, Deedie, I'm—sorry, but that's just the way I—uh—"

" 'Boy!' " said I. " 'This shall not excuse the injuries/ That thou hast done me; therefore turn and draw.' "

But since he was on one end of the phone and I was on the other and I couldn't reach him even if I had a pencil I just hung up.

28

Mr. Zachary was hardly ever absent from School and when he was, we knew it was something important. But a lot of other Teachers took off for Rest and Recreation, otherwise known as a Mental Health Day to regain their Sanity. Mrs. Vail for instance got sick every Wednesday so she could attend a Matinee in the City.

And when a Teacher was absent it was always a Cause for a Celebration because then we got a Substitute which meant we could talk all Period or write Notes to each other. Or as in the case of Mr. Harkavy, my Health Teacher, the boys threw the books out the window. I told you how the boys threatened to throw Mr. Harkavy out the window, which naturally they never did, but when Mr. Harkavy was absent they threw the books out the window so it wasn't a Total Loss.

But we never did that in Mr. Zachary's Class. First of all he said that a Substitute was really his own Personal Representative and deserved the same Respect and Consideration we gave him, and he would be Personally Insulted if we didn't behave. Also he would of murdered us.

But one day around the middle of March Mr. Zachary was absent and they couldn't get a Substitute, so Mrs. Ingleholtz had to take his Classes. Ordinarily we would of been disappointed with a Substitute in there, but it was a different story getting Mrs. Ingleholtz. If you remember, she was the Guidance Counselor who kept us posted on Robberies and recent Break-Ins, and Ax-Murders and stuff. So when we saw Mrs. Ingleholtz sitting at Mr. Zachary's desk with this long face, we naturally figured we'd spend the Period discussing the Theft of an Atom Bomb, or at least the latest Dismemberment Case.

Instead Mrs. Ingleholtz told us Mr. Zachary had to go to the Hospital to see his Wife.

"How long will he be out?"

"God knows," said Mrs. Ingleholtz.

We waited for her to say more but she didn't.

"Is his wife sick?"

"No one goes to the Hospital for a Vacation," said Mrs. Ingleholtz.

"Did she have another Baby?"

Mrs. Ingleholtz pressed her lips together. "I wish it were that simple," she said.

"Then what's the matter with her?"

I felt like we were playing Twenty Questions.

"She had an Operation," said Mrs. Ingleholtz.

We waited some more.

"Very Serious," said Mrs. Ingleholtz.

That scared us and we kept quiet. Mrs. Ingleholtz must of thought we were Giving Up. Her face got even longer.

"*Very* Serious," she said. "Yes, his wife had a Mastectomy so don't make trouble for me today because I'm out of my mind with Worry."

We looked at each other. To tell the truth I think the rest of the Class thought like I did, that it had something to do with Mastoids. But Mrs. Ingleholtz wanted to set us straight on that so she cleared her throat a couple of times and explained that a Mastectomy was when a Woman's Breast was removed which was nothing to sneeze at so would we please Cooperate for the next couple of days because she didn't want to have to Contend with any Behavior Problems and that was absolutely all she would say on the Subject and we shouldn't ask any further Questions.

We didn't, so Mrs. Ingleholtz spent the rest of the Period telling us how many of her friends died from the same thing but we shouldn't Worry because we were much too young to Concern ourselves, we would learn soon enough what a Lousy World this is and by that time the bell rang and we filed out of the room.

Nobody talked to anybody else. For some reason we all felt Guilty.

That night I asked Mom what she knew about Mastectomies.

"Why?" Mom said. "Are you Worried about something?"

"I guess," I said.

Mom got very white all of a sudden. "Come up to the bedroom," she said. "I want to look at you." She could hardly talk.

"Not me," I said. "Mrs. Zachary. She's in the Hospital."

"Oh," Mom said.

"Do people die from that?" I said.

"It's a Lousy World," Mom said.

"I know," I said.

"But it's wrong for Mr. Zachary to talk about his Personal Problems," Mom said.

"He didn't tell us," I said. "Mrs. Ingleholtz told us."

"Still and all," Mom said.

"Can she die from that?" I said.

"Teachers shouldn't talk about their Personal Problems," Mom said.

I don't agree. Kids should know that Teachers have Problems too. I mean when you're little you never think of them as being Human. Like having Families, or eating, or even going to the Bathroom.

Or shopping. I remember once when I was in First Grade I was with Mom in King Kullen and I saw this Teacher from my School. She smiled at me and said Hello and I almost died I was so embarrassed. Mom told me to say Hello back but I looked the other way. Finally the Teacher put this big roll of Toilet Paper in her shopping cart and walked up the aisle.

"Who was that?" Mom said.

"A Teacher," I said.

"Why didn't you talk to her?" Mom said.

"She's not *my* Teacher," I said.

"So?" Mom said.

"Why is she here anyway?" I said. I was very annoyed.

"Shopping of course," Mom said.

"She shops?" It was a big surprise to me.

So I don't think Mrs. Ingleholtz was wrong to tell us about Mrs. Zachary's Mastectomy. Except for the next three days we also found out about

Lobotomies, Vasectomies, and Hysterectomies (the only one I didn't have to Worry about was the middle one). Then she told us: we were being slowly poisoned by everything we took into our bodies; the clothes on our backs were loaded with Carcinogens which we'll surely discover the next time we break out in a Rash we thought all along was an Allergy; and on top of that we shouldn't forget how you could go to your Doctor for a Physical, get a Clean Bill of Health, and drop dead before you walked out of his Office (after you paid him a lot of money of course).

Mrs. Ingleholtz was right. It was a Lousy World.

Therefore we were very relieved when Mr. Zachary came back on the fourth day and he was all smiles.

"Hey!" he said. "I *missed* you!"

"Us too," we said. But we talked in whispers like we were at a Funeral.

"What's the matter?" Mr. Zachary said.

"Is your wife okay?" Paul said.

Mr. Zachary opened his eyes wide. "How'd you know about that?"

"Mrs. Ingleholtz told us," Paul said.

Mr. Zachary mumbled something about the Voice of Doom.

"Well she's fine," he said. When we didn't say

anything he said, "Really, Mrs. Zachary is *fine*! And it's very nice of you to be Concerned. Thank you."

"Were you scared?" Joey Falcaro said.

"Yes," Mr. Zachary said. "Yes I was."

"Because my Mother had the same thing and me and my Father were sure scared," Joey Falcaro said.

Everybody was surprised to hear that about Joey Falcaro's Mother. (Me especially. The sickest Mom ever got was a bad cold. Or a backache once. And even that scared me.)

Mr. Zachary's voice was real gentle. "How's your Mom now, Joey?"

"Oh, she's okay too," Joey Falcaro said. "And she said I should tell you not to Worry. If you want, she'll call up your wife and talk to her. I'm supposed to tell you that also."

I don't think I ever saw Mr. Zachary's eyes look so blue.

"I'd like that very much, Joey," Mr. Zachary said. "I'll give you the information before you leave today, okay?"

Maybe it wasn't such a Lousy World after all. I was even sorry I'd hung up on Joey Falcaro.

Then Paul said he was scared when his Father had a Heart Attack and Holly said that Heart Attacks ran in her Family but they didn't scare her as much as getting Kidnaped and the next thing you knew everybody was talking about what scared them the most and whose scary thing was more scary than anybody else's.

I kept thinking about Ritchie, and me being a Two-In-One and all of a sudden I remembered that Mother's Day was coming in a couple of months and more than anything I wanted to ask if anybody was scared of that but I knew how dumb that would sound.

Finally Mr. Zachary held up his hand which meant we should shut up. "Hold it," he said. "Is there anyone in this room who *isn't* Worried about something?"

Nobody raised a hand.

"Paul," Mr. Zachary said, "what's on your mind today? What are you Worried about right this minute?"

"The Soccer game this afternoon!" Paul said.

"Mm-hm," Mr. Zachary said. "What about you, Trish?"

Trish thought for a minute. "Well . . . my Grandmother's sick. My Father had to go see her last night."

"And you, Gina?" Mr. Zachary said.

Gina said, "I'm Worried about my Father. My Parents got Divorced last year."

"And you're afraid you won't see him again?" Mr. Zachary said.

Gina laughed. "I'm afraid I will!"

Mr. Zachary laughed too. "Well you're honest, Gina. How about you, Deedie?"

I shrugged my shoulders. "Little things," I said.

"Okay," Mr. Zachary said. "Here's what you're going to do. I want each of you to give a lot of thought to every single Worry you have. Big or small. Then I want you to list them on a sheet of paper."

"Why?"

"Because Worry is Emotion," Mr. Zachary said. "And Logic is Intelligence. I'd like you to use your Intelligence now instead of your Emotions. Let's see if we can eliminate the little problems that keep you from doing something constructive about the big ones. Shall we try that?"

"Did you make a List when you were Worried about your wife's Operation?"

"I did," Mr. Zachary said.

"So what good did it do?" Gina said. "She still had the Operation."

"True," Mr. Zachary said. "My list couldn't change that. But I had so many *little* Worries tacked on to the big one that I couldn't see the forest for the trees. I had to discover just which ones I could do something about."

"What are we supposed to do with the List?"

"Well the first thing I want you to do is to make

sure it's complete. Don't leave anything out, even if you think someone else will think it's silly. Get every one of your Worries out of your system and down on that piece of paper."

"Do we show them to you?"

"Nope! You're not going to show them to *anyone*! That way you won't be afraid to take those little buggers out for an airing and have a talk with them. And let 'em know you mean business! They've been in control so far, haven't they? Now *you're* going to show them who's Boss!"

"How do we do that?"

"By tackling them one at a time," Mr. Zachary said. "Divide and conquer, that's the strategy. And get the weaker ones out of the way first. Are you Worried about a Test? Then *study* for that Test! *Do* something about that Worry! Stop fussing, and act! When you finally come across one you can't handle, look for the cause. Nine times out of ten you'll find it's still you. Now get busy, everybody. And be tough on yourselves!"

I wrote my Worry List that night. Maybe you recall I actually started it in First Grade.

It was just a question of bringing it up to date.

29

Deedie Wooster
English

Mr. Zachary
Period 4

My Worry List

1- Mother's Day. Geranium! (Ugh)
2- If I don't buy one will Mom carry on like a Lunatic? Is Mom a Lunatic?
3- Which does Mom really love? Me or the Geranium?
4- Does Mom even like me?
5- What if I get my Period when I'm in School and I don't have a Nickel for the machine?
6- When is my next Doctor's Appointment?

7- Will Russia drop an Atom Bomb on New Jersey in the middle of the night?
8- Will Joey Falcaro call me Piano Legs again?
9- What if the Six o'clock News shows the Baby Seals getting Clubbed to Death?
10- Will our Nuclear Plant Spring a Leak?
11- What will the Library do if I lost a Book?
12- Is it safe to start any Long Term Projects? (I am two years past Twelve.)
13- Why doesn't J. F. call me P. L. anymore?
14- Could Geraniums be Hazardous to my Health?
15- Geraniums!
16- Two-In-One!!!
17- Mother's Day!!! Ugh!!!!!

I got some thumbtacks and put my Worry List on the inside of my closet door. I took my terry-cloth bathrobe and hung it inside the door so that it covered my Worry List.

I completely forgot that Mom sometimes took my bathrobe down to wash it.

Wait a second. This is the *end* of my Book not the beginning. I'm a big girl now.

I knew Mom would do a laundry in the morning.

30

Do you remember I told you I would of liked a big Climax in the last Chapter? Well the reason I'm reminding you of that now is because this part of my book is that part of my book, if you know what I mean. Right here is where you should be sitting on the edge of your chair chewing your nails and if you got a phone call you'd have to say:

"Listen, I can't talk to you now because Deedie Wooster is about to get Clobbered by her Mother! I'll get back to you in about ten minutes, I promise!"

Forget it. Go right ahead and take your call.

Because nothing happened.

I mean I knew Mom saw my Worry List. My bathrobe had been washed and hung back up inside my closet door when I came home from

School. But Mom didn't greet me at the door with my Worry List quivering in her hand. She only said Hello and told me to make my bed and then she said that Joey Falcaro had called a couple of minutes before I got home to say he was coming over and who was Joey Falcaro anyway?

"Some Creep," I said.

So Mom said, Well, he sounded like a little Gentleman to her, and I said she was right about the first part, and she said there were Chocolate Grahams in the breadbox but I should save some of the milk for Daddy's coffee. I didn't think it was an Opportune Time to tell her that the kids in my School didn't snack on Chocolate Grahams, they filled up their tanks on Seagram's Seven, so I just said Thanks and went up to my room to review the Situation.

And I want to say right now that you could of knocked me over with a feather. Not that Joey Falcaro was coming over because he'd been threatening to do that for weeks. I'd just been telling him to stick his head in a bucket if he could find one big enough which I doubted. But I was so surprised that Mom didn't mention my Worry List that I didn't even have time to think up any nasty Quotes to hit him with.

If you want to know the afternoon was full of surprises, because not only did Joey Falcaro prefer

Chocolate Grahams to Seagram's Seven, he actually ate them the way I did when I was little. You know, sticking his finger in his mouth so he could pick every single crumb off the table. After he polished off a whole box that way we went up to my room to listen to Albums. I made him wash his hands first.

When he finally left, I figured *Here it comes!* but Mom still didn't say anything except to comment that it was Improper to Entertain a Boy (even if the Boy *is* a Gentleman) in my Bedroom when we had a perfectly adequate Living Room in this house. I would of explained that our Living Room would of been more adequate minus approx. one doz. Geraniums but I assumed that any minute she would bring up the subject of Geraniums herself. She didn't.

So I helped with the Dinner dishes (without being asked for the first time in my life) and said I had to do my Homework but I really wanted to check my bathrobe again.

Sure enough it had been washed.

Now, you know how sometimes when you're riding your bicycle you see a hole in the road and you know you'd better not ride over the hole or your bike will skid? And for some crazy reason you aim right for that hole and land on your head? What I mean is, when I saw for *sure* my bathrobe had been washed, you'd think I would of kept my mouth shut and waited for Events to take their Natural Course. But no, just like that Four-Color Ball-Point pen business, and my pretend sister Eleanor, and Kristy McNichol, *I* had to go back downstairs again to where Mom and Daddy were now sitting in front of the TV.

"Thanks for washing my bathrobe," I said.

(I ask you, was that dumb or was it dumb?)

But it was like the subj. of Ger. was a Closed Book.

"You're Welcome," Mom said.

"I could of done it," I said.

"That's okay," Mom said. "I had to do a Laundry anyway."

"I know," I said.

"I *know* you know," said Mom.

"?" thought I.

For ten minutes or so I dusted around the Geraniums till Mom told me to light someplace, so I flopped down on the couch and pretended to watch this Documentary on Abused Children in which Mom was fanatically engrossed at the moment. Daddy was dozing.

I made a little Chit-Chat about the Program but Mom didn't seem to hear me so I threw out the Casual Observation that *some* kids, like *me,* for instance, didn't know when they were Well Off, and Mom threw back the Casual Observation that she supposed so, and I said, Well, I *know* so, and Mom threw out the Casual Observation that I'd do her a big favor if I kept quiet because she couldn't hear the Commentator. The air was full of Casual Observations.

I threw out another one when I said, "The Geraniums need watering."

Mom's last C.O. was that they *always* did.

Then I went back upstairs and that's when I really started to Worry. I figured maybe Mom would *never* say anything about that List, maybe she would just call the School and have Mr. Zachary fired, or at least make them transfer me to another English Class where they were Getting Down To The Basics.

But that didn't happen either. Days passed, then weeks. To tell the truth I hated to think about my Worry List after that first day. I'd torn it down from my closet door and stuck it away in my desk. But one day, about a month later, I took it out again.

Mr. Zachary had said: *Tackle them one at a time. Do something about that Worry! Stop fussing, and act!*

I went down the List. I hadn't realized how silly some of those Worries looked on paper. I stopped fussing and began to act. I wrote a Protest Letter about the Baby Seals getting Clubbed to Death, addressed it to a TV Station, and mailed it. That made me feel a little better so after I saw *The China Syndrome* with Joey Falcaro I wrote another Protest Letter on Nuclear Plants, made him sign it too, and we mailed it together. He supplied the Stamp.

I searched for the lost Library book, found it in the back of my closet under my Monopoly Game, and took it back to the Library. The Librarian didn't call the cops as I expected. She only smiled and said "Thank you," then charged me the Maximum: three dollars.

I even taped a nickel under the torn lining in my pocketbook. I could get my Period every day for the rest of my life (ugh!) but at least I'd be Prepared.

One by one I crossed them off.

Then finally I had to face those last few Worries on my List.

Geraniums. Two-In-One. Mother's Day.

I thought about Words again. Combinations of letters, Mr. Zachary said. Symbols. They meant only what you wanted them to mean. Saying "I love you" didn't mean anything unless *you* meant it. Words had to have meaning or they were meaningless.

I'd been using Words all wrong. I'd thought I

was a Dilly Dally because that Teacher said I was. But I wasn't a Dilly Dally. I only dilly-dallied. I wasn't a Dawdler. I only dawdled.

There were different kinds of capitals too.

I looked again at some of the things I'd crossed out.

Piano Legs. *Piano Legs?* Oh, come *on,* Deedie, do you really have piano legs? A cowlick, yes. But not piano legs.

Then what was Joey Falcaro trying to say?

He was using a symbol. Maybe the symbol meant "I like you a little, Deedie Wooster!" Was that so *improbable*?

Then the geranium was a symbol too. I'd tried to pretend it was Mom's, but it wasn't. It was mine. *I'd* chosen it. Each time I'd given Mom that geranium I was saying, "Love *me,* Mom. Love *me*!" I'd been trying to take Ritchie's place.

I'd made myself the Two-In-One.

People grow up in spurts, I think. I felt a little spurt the day I realized I hadn't really caught a bird in the palm of my hand. I felt another one when it dawned on me that Mrs. Reif knew it too.

And I felt it again when I knew I hadn't written that worry list for me. How much simpler it would of been if . . . no, let me start that sentence over —I just felt another spurt. How much simpler it would *have* been if a long, long time ago I'd said,

"I know you love me, Mom. And I don't need to bring you any more geraniums."

And a funny thought occurs to me now. When I say "funny" I mean strange, you understand. I'm wondering if maybe the fact that my book doesn't have a climax means there really is a climax after all. Maybe the climax is that nothing happened, nothing that anyone could see.

It was only something inside of me.

31

I wasn't going to bring Mom a geranium for Mother's Day. I bought some flower seeds in the supermarket, planted them in four little milk cartons, and put them on the windowsill in my room. There was a picture of the flowers on the package but that wasn't why I chose them. I liked the name.

The seeds didn't sprout at first. I thought maybe I did something wrong. Then one day I saw a little bit of green sticking up from the dirt. I was so happy I felt like crying. It must be like seeing your new baby for the first time.

I watched the seeds grow into seedlings. Then almost overnight they got too big for the containers. I knew they needed room to grow. If I left them where they were they would have withered and died. People are like that too. Every living thing needs room to grow.

I looked the four plants over real carefully because I wanted to keep only one. Three of them were pretty healthy, but the one on the end was having a tough time keeping its stem straight. It had been stuck behind my curtain and didn't get enough sun. The stem reminded me of a little green cowlick. It was kind of scrawny and sad-looking. Naturally that's the one I kept.

The next day I brought the other three plants to school. I gave one to Dennis and one to Heather who told me she was on her way to Long Island for a week.

"That's not too far," I said.

"I'm sticking closer to home," Heather said. "Can I have Allie's?"

That's when I found out Allie was never coming back. I wondered if I'd given Allie Mom's pills if it would have made any difference. I didn't think so though.

I took special care of the plant I kept. By Mother's Day it still looked like it could have used a double dose of cod liver oil and calcium tablets but it was alive and growing and I knew it would be all right. I brought it downstairs to Mom.

"It's a forget-me-not," I said.

"Really?" Mom said. "It'll be lovely when it comes up."

I looked at the forget-me-not, then back at Mom.

"It *is* up!" I said.

Mom laughed and took the forget-me-not.

"No geranium?" Mom said.

"No geranium," I said.

Then she smiled. A smile is better than a laugh, sometimes. She looked at the forget-me-not, then she looked at me. A long time.

"You're right," Mom said. "It *is* up."

I gave her the card.

Dear Mom,
I love you enough for the two of us.
Love, Deedie

When the weather got warm I made a flower-bed in the backyard near our fence. The forget-me-not looked kind of lonely all by itself in the flower-bed. I knew I'd made the flower-bed too big on purpose anyway.

I went to a florist and bought a geranium. I thought maybe that florist would have heard bells ring or something when I asked for the geranium, but he just gave it to me and I paid him. The bells did ring except they were inside me, and as long as I heard them it didn't matter that no one else did.

I left the geranium in the pot and dug another hole in the flower-bed next to Mom's forget-me-not. Before I stuck it in the ground, I put a little mark on the side of the pot. It was a special geranium because it was the only one I ever really wanted to buy. I had to be able to tell it apart from the others.

It's the end of August now and I know that pretty soon the forget-me-not will die. It doesn't matter because next year I'll buy more seeds and plant them all over again. I love to watch things grow from seeds. But I'll bring my geranium into the house in a few weeks.

Before the first frost.

32

Epilogue

" 'O, wilt thou leave me so unsatisfied?' "

In case you think it was me who said that, it wasn't, it was Joey Falcaro. He'd been driving me crazy with that stuff all summer.

" 'What satisfaction canst thou have tonight?' " I said.

"Heh, heh," said he.

"Heh, heh, yourself," said I.

I tried to raise my eyebrow and still couldn't. But it would have been a wasted effort anyway. We were sitting on the patio in my backyard, and it's very dark there.

"What's that funny smell?" Joey Falcaro said.

"Chocolate Grahams," I said.

"No," he said, "I mean that other smell."

"Oh," I said. "Geraniums."

"They stink," he said.

I said, " 'A rose by any other na—' "

"Yeah, yeah," said Joey Falcaro. "We going bike riding in the morning?"

"Okay," I said. "What time?"

" 'At the hour of nine,' " he said.

"Put a lid on it," I said.

Mom stuck her head out the window. "Deedie!" she yelled.

" 'I come anon!' " I said.

I walked Joey Falcaro to the gate.

" 'Good night, good night,' " I said. " 'Parting is such—' "

"Less talk, Piano Legs," he said. "You got a big mouth."

"I do not!" I said.

" 'No,' " said Joey Falcaro, " ' 'tis not so deep as a well, nor so wide as a church door; but 'tis enough, 'twill serve.' "

He was definitely getting too good for me.

"I have to go in," I said.

" 'Sleep dwell upon thine eyes, peace in thy breast!' " he said, and shoved his hands under my NOBODY'S PREFECT T-shirt.

"Uh-*uh*!" I said. "Not *there*!"

"I'm quoting," said Joey Falcaro.

"Well, you can't quote there," I said.

He leaned against me and nailed me to the gate.

I said, " 'I have a faint cold fear thrills through my veins—' "

He put his hand over my mouth.

"Do you wanna?" he said.

"Only if you wanna," I said, which was exactly how I felt.

He kissed me. I didn't have to bend my legs as much as the last time. His mouth was nearly level with mine now. Joey Falcaro was growing faster than my forget-me-nots.

We had to close our eyes so they didn't cross.

"Deedie!" Mom screamed.

" 'It is the lark that sings so out of tune,' " said Joey Falcaro.

He kissed me again so I kissed him back. We kissed a long time. I didn't hold my breath. I breathed in as much as I breathed out.

" 'Thou hast amazed me,' " whispered Joey Falcaro.

To tell the truth, I didst myself.

I licked the Chocolate Grahams off my lips and straightened my NOBODY'S PREFECT T-shirt. It was definitely losing its shape after all.

About the Author

Anita Jacobs was born in New York City and attended Brooklyn College and Hofstra University. A teacher of ninth-grade English, she lives with her family in Wantagh, New York. *Where Has Deedie Wooster Been All These Years?* is her first novel.